The Hypersonic Secret

The pilot gave a firm salute. Then he clamped the satchel handle between his teeth and jumped out of the plane.

Joe ran to the door and watched him plummet through the air. A moment later the parachute billowed open, and the pilot was floating safely toward the ground.

Just then the Hardys were sent reeling as the plane began nosing steeply downward. Joe grabbed the doorframe to keep from falling out. As the wind roared against his face, Joe saw the sandy brown surface of the desert rushing closer.

"Do something!" Joe yelled. "We're crashing!"

"I've got no control device!" Frank yelled.

As the plane dove downward, Joe glanced out the door again. His stomach somersaulted as he saw the harsh face of the desert rushing up to meet them. . . .

The Hardy Boys Mystery Stories

Available from MINSTREL Books

THE HARDY BOYS® MYSTERY STORIES

135

The HARDY BOYS®

THE HYPERSONIC SECRET

FRANKLIN W. DIXON

A
MINSTREL®
BOOK

Published by POCKET BOOKS
New York   London   Toronto   Sydney   Tokyo   Singapore

A MINSTREL PAPERBACK *Original*

A Minstrel Book published by
POCKET BOOKS, a division of Simon & Schuster Inc.
1230 Avenue of the Americas, New York, NY 10020

Copyright © 1995 by Simon & Schuster Inc.

Front cover illustration by Brian Kotzky

Produced by Mega-Books, Inc.

ISBN: 0-671-50518-1

First Minstrel Books printing December 1995

10 9 8 7 6 5 4 3 2 1

THE HARDY BOYS MYSTERY STORIES is a trademark of Simon & Schuster Inc.

THE HARDY BOYS, A MINSTREL BOOK and colophon are registered trademarks of Simon & Schuster Inc.

Printed in the U.S.A.

Contents

1 Vanished

Frank Hardy gripped the control wheel of a 727 passenger jet. "Okay," he said, "let's bring this big guy down."

"Altitude twenty thousand feet," Frank's brother, Joe, said from the copilot's chair. Joe's blue eyes were glued to the dials of the airplane's instrument panel.

"Phoenix tower." Frank spoke into the mike on his headset. "This is six-six-eight-niner-Juliet. I'm at twenty thousand feet over Rio Verde, and I'm requesting approach clearance for landing in Phoenix."

As a response from the tower came through his headset, Frank admired the perfectly blue sky through the windshield. A thousand feet below, a layer of clouds floated on the air like a fluffy blanket.

"Cut back the throttles," Frank told Joe as he began easing the wheel forward. Immediately, Frank felt the giant plane angling downward.

"Flying a 727's not so tough," Joe boasted as he gently pulled back on all three power levers. Blond, muscular, and six foot tall, Joe Hardy felt as if he could handle just about anything in the big jet's cockpit.

"Don't count your chickens before the plane's on the ground," Frank advised. At eighteen, dark-haired Frank was an inch taller and a year older than his brother. He was also the more cautious of the two Hardys. "The most dangerous part of a flight," Frank continued, "is always the last few—"

Suddenly the wheel began vibrating in Frank's hand. A red light flashed on the instrument panel and a high-pitched "whoop whoop" alarm filled the cabin.

"What's happening?" Joe asked, instantly on full alert.

"I don't know," Frank replied, his brown eyes scanning the instrument panel.

The plane started shaking and rumbling, and the Hardys were jolted against their safety straps.

"I think we've stalled," Frank announced tensely as he pushed hard on the control wheel.

"What happens now?" Joe asked. He had to work to keep his voice steady.

Then he got his answer. The nose of the plane

2

dipped, and the aircraft zoomed straight through the layer of clouds. Joe watched helplessly as the altimeter dial began spinning around too fast for him to monitor.

"We're diving!" Frank cried, jerking back the control wheel. "Close the throttles!"

Joe yanked the power levers all the way back. The wheel stopped vibrating, and the red light went off, but the plane continued plummeting at a frightening speed.

"Hardy brothers," a voice behind Frank and Joe said, "it looks like we've got an emergency situation."

Frank glanced over his right shoulder at seventeen-year-old Jamal Hawkins, who was sitting in the flight engineer chair directly behind Joe. Jamal's dark eyes flashed as if he was relishing the sudden danger at hand.

"The most important thing to remember in a flight crisis," Jamal told them, "is to stay cool. If you can do that, chances are you'll save the day."

"Okay, okay, we're cool," Joe said, watching the clouds rush by the windshield. "Now what?"

"Frank," Jamal instructed calmly, "ease back the wheel very, very gently. If you're too fast, you could snap off a wing. Joe, as the plane begins leveling off, ease those throttles open again."

Mustering all the cool he had, Frank gently pulled back on the control wheel. Seconds later Frank was glad to feel the airplane settle back into its horizontal position.

3

"You caught a bad angle," Jamal explained, "so you stalled. The vibrating wheel and the red light were trying to warn you, but you were too slow reacting. Understandable considering you boys have never flown a big bird like this before."

Ten minutes later Frank brought the 727 gliding down to a near perfect landing. As Frank shut off the jet engines, he and Joe each let out a big sigh of relief.

"These flight simulators are pretty realistic," Frank said. "I could swear I just landed a real 727 at the Phoenix airport."

Jamal and the Hardys left the model cockpit, thanked a man at a computer console, and climbed down a ladder. The boys were not really in Phoenix but in a large flight training room at the Bayport Airport. Above them stood the big white chamber of a flight simulator. Using computerized images and hydraulic motion, the simulator could vividly re-create the experience of flying a genuine airplane.

"Those are great for training pilots," Frank observed. "Especially for emergency situations."

"We should get one for the garage," Joe joked.

"They only cost a few mil," Jamal said.

"Put it on your Christmas list," Frank suggested with a grin.

"He'd have to have been awfully good this year," Jamal quipped. "Hard to imagine."

Frank laughed along with his new friend. Jamal Hawkins was a few inches shorter than the Hardys, and though slender in build, he was in top condition. Joe had discovered exactly how fit his friend was during the football game the previous Friday night. Jamal, playing for a nearby school, had given Bayport a run for their money.

After the game, which Bayport High lost, the Hardys made it a point to congratulate Jamal on his performance. When Jamal discovered Frank had a pilot's license, he invited the Hardys out for a day at the airport. Jamal's father owned an air-taxi service, and Jamal spent much of his time at the Bayport Airport.

"Let's pay a visit to the control tower," Jamal said as he and the Hardys put on their heavy coats. "Then I'll show you my dad's planes."

As soon as the three friends stepped through a door, they were blasted by a gust of wintry wind.

"Brrr," Joe said, pulling up his hood.

"It's supposed to snow tonight," Frank said, zipping up his coat. He noticed the late afternoon sky was gray and laced with clouds.

The boys headed toward a tower that rose high over the airport grounds. It was six days before Christmas, and the place was buzzing with activity. The parked jets were being serviced by small armies of people, equipment, and trucks. Off on a runway, a 727 thundered up into the sky.

"How many planes does your dad have in his air-taxi fleet?" Joe yelled over the surrounding noise.

"Seven," Jamal yelled back. "All of them are lightplanes. That means two, four, and six seaters."

5

"Is it mostly businesspeople who charter them?" Frank asked loudly.

"Pretty much," Jamal answered. "Either they need to get somewhere out of the way or they just don't want the hassle of a commercial flight."

"Does your dad fly many clients himself?" Joe asked.

"No, he usually stays in the hangar to run things," Jamal said. "He did fly a client to Ottawa today, but he should be back by now. As soon as we're done at the tower, I'll take you to meet him."

The boys entered the tower building, rode an elevator up ten stories, then stepped into the air traffic control room. It was a large circular room with windows that showed a panoramic view of the airport and the ocean beyond. Three people with headsets were seated at a console that ran all the way around the perimeter of the room. The controllers were all efficiently at work—watching the planes, speaking to pilots, and monitoring radar screens.

"The nerve center of the airport," Jamal announced.

"How's it going, Jamal?" one of the controllers asked, keeping her eyes on a dark green radar screen.

"Pretty fair," Jamal replied. "Say, Lonnie, my dad was supposed to return from Ottawa about an hour ago. Do you know if he's back yet?"

"I haven't seen him come in," Lonnie answered.

6

"Why don't you call down to Approach Control and see what they can tell you."

"I really want you guys to meet my dad," Jamal told the Hardys as he picked up a phone receiver. "Pilot and father extraordinaire." Frank remembered that it was just Jamal and his dad. Jamal's mom had died a number of years before.

As Jamal began speaking on the phone, Joe gazed out the circular windows. Dusk was falling across the airport, and tiny lights were now glowing along the runways. A 767 zoomed down from the sky and smoothly rushed along a runway.

Frank and Joe wandered about the room, watching airplanes come and go in every direction. Joe noticed each of the planes was being directed by the calm voice of one of the controllers in the room.

"The controllers up here just guide the planes in and out of the airport area, right?" Joe asked.

"Right," Frank said. "Then controllers on the ground floor take over for a number of miles. Next the planes are passed off to enroute controllers who are scattered at centers across the country. The pilot always has someone to help him if he needs it."

After a few minutes of watching the controllers in action, Frank looked back at Jamal, who was still on the phone. But now his friend had a stunned expression on his face. Frank gave Joe a nudge and nodded toward Jamal.

The Hardys watched Jamal set down the phone

7

and move like a zombie to a section of the window. Frank and Joe walked over to join him.

"Jamal, what is it?" Frank asked with concern. "Is something wrong?"

Jamal kept staring through the glass of the panoramic window. It was almost dark now, and a light snow had begun drifting down from the sky.

"My dad's plane is missing," Jamal said finally.

"Missing?" Joe asked. "What do you mean?"

"The plane left Ottawa on schedule," Jamal reported. "But a little later an enroute controller was tracking the plane's course on radar over the Adirondack mountains in upstate New York. The plane suddenly disappeared on the radar screen. It was like my dad's plane just . . . vanished."

2 Out of the Picture

For a long moment the boys stared out the window, forgetting about the people and voices around them. In silence, they watched as the snow continued to drift through the darkening sky.

"Well, there's probably a good explanation," Joe finally said. "We just have to find out what it is."

"Your dad is an experienced pilot," Frank added. "If his plane were malfunctioning, he would have sent a Mayday to the controller following him."

"That's right," Jamal said, worry written all over his face. "But my dad's plane disappeared on the radar over three hours ago, and apparently nobody has received a Mayday from the plane."

"Even if the plane did go down," Joe said, "don't all planes have some sort of tracking device?"

"It's called an ELT," Jamal explained. "Emer-

9

gency locator transmitter. Every airplane has one, and it automatically sends out radio signals when the plane hits the ground. That way the plane can be tracked to its exact location. But so far no one has picked up an ELT signal from my dad's plane."

"No Mayday call and no ELT signal," Frank said, his mind struggling for a simple answer. "This is very strange."

"I know," Jamal agreed. "It's like the plane just vanished. If my dad's radio was working, or if he could get to a phone, he'd have contacted the office to explain why he was late. He's very careful about that. But I just called the hangar, and they haven't heard from him."

"What's being done to find the plane?" Joe asked.

"The Civil Air Patrol has already started a search," Jamal explained. "They're flying over the area where the plane disappeared and, if it's there, they should find it eventually. But the mountains will make the search difficult. I'm, uh . . . I'm going to go to my dad's office to wait for news. Do you guys want to come or do you have to get going?"

"We're staying with you," Joe said, clasping Jamal's shoulder. "We'll stay with you until we know exactly where your father is."

"Thanks," Jamal said, obviously grateful.

Jamal and the Hardys left the tower and hurried across the airport grounds. It was now completely dark outside, and the boys put their hoods up to ward off the falling snow.

They came to a group of airplane hangars made of corrugated steel. Above one of the hangars a sign announced Hawkins Air Service.

"This is my dad's place," Jamal said, leading the Hardys through a door in the side of the hangar.

Two lightplanes were parked inside the spacious hangar, and a mechanic in blue coveralls was doing repair work on one of them. Fluorescent lights shone from the high ceiling, and space heaters managed to give the place some warmth.

At the front of the hangar were some folding metal chairs and a cluttered desk. A young woman was going through some papers at the desk. She had messy red hair and wore an extra large sweater over stretch pants. When the woman saw Jamal, she rushed right over to him.

"Oh, Jamal!" the woman cried, giving him a big hug. "I just *know* your father's all right. He's the best."

"Frank, Joe, meet Betty Perkins," Jamal said with a slight smile. "She's secretary, receptionist, and general morale booster around here."

"It's a pleasure," Betty said. "I just wish it were under better circumstances."

"Listen, Betty," Jamal said, "who was the passenger on Dad's flight today?"

"Well . . ." Betty glanced at Frank and Joe. "I'm not really supposed to say."

"It's okay," Jamal assured her. "Who was it?"

11

"Mr. Hawkins had only one passenger on the plane," Betty answered. "Ian Fairbanks."

"*The* Ian Fairbanks?" Joe was surprised. "The British millionaire who owns the chain of Fairbanks department stores?"

"That's the one," Betty said. "Apparently Mr. Fairbanks likes to keep his comings and goings private, so he asked us not to announce he was flying with us."

"Fairbanks is incredibly wealthy," Frank commented. "I'm surprised he doesn't have his own plane and pilot to fly him around."

"He does," Betty said. "But it seems his plane developed a problem, so he called us yesterday to book a flight. All the pilots already had flights scheduled, so Mr. Hawkins agreed to fly him."

"Does Fairbanks live around here?" Joe asked.

"No," Frank answered. "But I've heard he's in town sometimes to check on the Bayport store."

"His daughter, Tamara, lives in Bayport, though," Betty explained. "She runs the local Fairbanks store. She's listed as the person to call in case of an emergency. I guess I'd better call her and explain the situation."

"This could be pretty upsetting for her," Jamal said. "I guess I should deliver the news in person."

"Why don't Joe and I go for you?" Frank suggested. "You stay here and wait for news. As soon as we're done, we'll meet you back here."

Frank could see that Jamal was grateful for the offer. "Thanks, man."

A few minutes later, Frank and Joe were driving their van through the evening traffic. The snow was falling a little harder now, turning the city white and hushed. Joe looked over at Frank. He seemed to be in his "deep thought" mode.

"What are you thinking?" Joe asked.

"Planes just don't vanish like that," Frank said. "If there was trouble, why didn't Mr. Hawkins radio someone? And if the plane went down, why didn't the ELT go off?"

"They're both electrical devices," Joe said. "Which means they can always go dead."

"But those two devices aren't connected," Frank explained. "The radio is part of the electrical system, and the ELT runs by battery. And the fact that both failed to operate is an awfully big coincidence."

"What are you driving at?" Joe asked. "That someone rigged that plane to go down? And rigged it so the devices wouldn't work?"

"There are two things I've heard about Ian Fairbanks," Frank said. "He's got millions of dollars and almost as many enemies."

"So you think this wasn't an accident," Joe said.

"It's possible," Frank said. "And for the sake of Jamal's father, I'd like to find out a little more about Mr. Fairbanks."

"No wonder you volunteered to see Tamara Fairbanks," Joe said, turning up the heat dial. "Good thinking."

When the Hardys arrived at the sprawling Fair-

13

banks department store, just after seven, the parking lot was jammed with cars. After circling awhile, Frank drove down a ramp and finally found a parking space in the underground garage.

Upstairs, the store swarmed with holiday shoppers. Music blared, and Joe could barely see Santa Claus through the long line of kids waiting to tell him what they wanted.

"Oh, no," Joe said, slapping his forehead. "We still haven't gotten Aunt Gertrude a Christmas present!"

"Maybe we can pick up something tomorrow," Frank said, scanning the store directory.

After riding an elevator to the top floor, the Hardys entered a plush office area. Frank told the receptionist they wanted to see Tamara Fairbanks. "We have news about her father," he explained.

"Let me check with her," the young woman said, picking up a phone.

Joe noticed a framed photograph on the wall behind her. The subject was a portly man in his early sixties with dark, bushy eyebrows that made him seem oddly comical and sinister at the same time.

"I guess that's Ian Fairbanks," Joe observed.

"Looks like he's watching us," Frank said, also studying the man's dark eyes.

"Ms. Fairbanks will see you now," the receptionist told the Hardys. "It's the last door down the hall."

14

At the end of a long hallway, the Hardys came to an oak door with the words *Tamara Fairbanks* engraved on a gold plate. The door was closed, but Frank and Joe could hear a female voice coming from the office. They listened closely.

"I know," a woman inside said in a British accent. "My father has been making it difficult for everybody. Most of all me. But if we can pull this thing off, the mighty Ian Fairbanks will be out of the picture for good. . . . Listen, we shouldn't talk about this over the phone. My chauffeur will be picking me up in the garage soon. Why don't I stop by your office and we'll go over some of the new ideas in person? Great. 'Bye."

Frank and Joe exchanged a look. They waited a moment, then Joe knocked at the door.

"Come in," the woman called.

The Hardys stepped inside an elegantly decorated office. Tamara Fairbanks sat behind a glass desk, holding a fountain pen in her hand. She was a striking woman in her late thirties with dark hair pulled tightly back. She wore a tailored black suit, and jewels glittered like ice on her fingers.

"Let's make this fast," Tamara Fairbanks ordered. "Rosalind said this was about my father."

"Ms. Fairbanks," Frank stated, "I'm afraid the airplane your father was on today is now missing." He went on to explain where the plane had disappeared on radar and what was being done to find it. As he spoke, he was careful to note how Ms.

Fairbanks took the news. He noticed she began to twirl the pen in her hand, but otherwise she had no reaction.

"I want you to know," Tamara said after Frank was done, "if this is due to negligence on the part of Hawkins Air Service, I will personally sue that company for everything they've got."

"It could have been a mechanical problem," Frank replied evenly, "but we're also wondering if there may have been some foul play."

Joe noticed Tamara started twirling the fountain pen again. "Do you know anyone who may have reason to harm your father?" he asked.

"Are you kidding?" Tamara scoffed. "There are countless people all over the world who would like to harm Ian Fairbanks. He's lied to and cheated practically every person he's ever met!"

"Can you be more specific," Joe prompted.

"No, I can't," Tamara said curtly.

"Do you know what your father was doing in Ottawa?" Frank asked.

"Who are you boys, anyway?" Tamara inquired as she leaned forward on the glass desk. "Do you work for Hawkins Air Service?"

"No," Joe answered. "We're friends of the owner's son."

"Oh, really?" Tamara said. Joe sensed some kind of accusation in her tone.

"Yes, really," Joe said, wondering what she was getting at. They stared at each other for a moment. Joe noticed she had her father's dark eyes.

16

"Well," Tamara said, the disdain in her voice unmistakable, "I really don't have time to sit around and chat with a couple of jocks in blue jeans. Please show yourselves out at once."

"We're sorry to have bothered you," Frank said. "We'll let you know as soon as we learn anything about your father. Good night."

The Hardys returned to the elevator and waited for the doors to close before they spoke. "I think Ms. Fairbanks just gave us our first suspect," Joe said. "Herself. What did she say on the phone? 'If we can pull this thing off, the mighty Ian Fairbanks will be out of the picture for good.'"

"Another thing," Frank added. "When we told her that her father was missing, she didn't show the slightest bit of emotion. Not exactly what you'd expect from a concerned daughter."

"I've got an idea," Joe said as the Hardys returned to their van in the underground garage. "Tamara said her chauffeur was picking her up down here, and then she was going to meet the person she was talking to on the phone. How about we follow and see where she leads us?"

"Sounds good to me," Frank agreed, opening the van door.

The Hardys parked just inside the exit of the garage and watched cars come and go. Soon a long black limousine pulled up at the underground store entrance.

"That must be it," Joe said, watching the limo.

Moments later Tamara Fairbanks stepped out of

the store wearing a long tan coat. A tall chauffeur in a black suit got out of the car and opened the back door for her.

"What a mug," Joe said. The chauffeur had a crew cut, a broken nose, and an especially mean face.

"Even uglier than you," Frank said, starting up the van.

The Hardys followed the limousine about five miles to a glass office building that had only a few lights still on. Because the parking lot was almost empty, Frank parked far from the building to escape notice.

Through the veil of falling snow, the Hardys watched Tamara step out of the limo and walk toward the building's entrance. The chauffeur drove the limo around the side of the building, soon disappearing from sight.

"Okay, she's in the building," Joe said. He and Frank jumped out of the van and started across the parking lot.

"We'll see what floor her elevator stops at from the overhead indicator," Frank said. "She's probably planning to be here awhile because the chauffeur didn't stay and wait."

"Frank, look," Joe said, a few steps later.

A black vehicle had come around the side of the building and was now approaching the Hardys at low speed. Weird, Joe thought, the guy's headlights are out. Through the darkness and drifting snow, it seemed like a strange, ambling monster.

18

"It's the limo," Frank whispered. "I wonder . . ."

Suddenly the limo's headlights flashed on. The car gunned its engine, then shot forward. Frank heard spinning tires and glimpsed a spray of snow in the air. The limo was roaring straight for them!

3 Collision Course

"He's after us!" Frank yelled.

Joe and Frank raced away from the limo, but they heard the car bearing down hard on their backs. They were running toward the van, but Frank knew there was no way they could beat the limo to it.

"Turn!" Frank shouted. Instantly Frank and Joe veered sharp to the left. Frank lost his footing on the turn and slipped to the ground. He heard the limo roar by, missing them by inches.

Frank sprang up and watched the limo make a sharp turn back toward him and Joe. In the slushy parking lot, the driver lost control and the limo narrowly missed a parked car. Frank glanced around, looking for cover, but there were no nearby cars for protection, and the building's entrance was a good distance away.

"He's coming back for us," Joe panted. With a roar, the limo shot forward again.

"Run for the van!" Frank yelled. "Maybe we can make it this time."

Frank concentrated on his footsteps in the snow. One slip now could prove fatal. As he neared the van, Frank pulled the keys from his pocket.

"Hurry!" Joe cried. He could hear the limo's deadly roar right behind him.

Frank quickly turned the key in the van door and yanked it open. Joe dove onto the front seat of the van, and Frank piled in after him. He saw the limo skid and fishtail dangerously close just as he yanked the door closed. The limo had avoided broadsiding the van by only a few inches.

"He's not a chauffeur," Frank exclaimed, locking the van door. "He's a maniac!"

Both Frank and Joe sat up on their seats to see what might be coming next. Through the falling snow, Joe could make out the face of the chauffeur. Anger shot through him when he saw the chauffeur's lips form into a smile.

"Maybe he just wanted to scare us away," Frank said, catching his breath.

"From what?" Joe wondered.

"That's for us to find out," Frank said as he stuck the ignition key in the van. "But later."

Frank drove the van out of the parking lot, glad to see that the chauffeur didn't follow them. With an eye on the rearview mirror, Frank drove back

21

toward the airport. Soon he and Joe returned to the Hawkins Air Service hangar.

The Hardys went through the side door of the hangar but found the place empty. "Jamal!" Joe called, his voice echoing under the steel roof.

"Back here," Jamal answered from the rear of the hangar.

Frank and Joe walked through the hangar and found their friend in the wood-paneled room that served as Mr. Hawkins's office. Jamal was sitting at his father's desk, and a young man wearing khakis and a leather flight jacket was standing by him.

"Any news?" Joe asked Jamal.

Jamal shook his head. "Ken and I have been glued to the phone, but so far there's been no word. Joe, Frank, meet Ken McCafferty. He's one of my dad's pilots."

"Good to meet you," Ken McCafferty said as he shook hands with each of the Hardys.

McCafferty was a tall, friendly fellow in his late twenties with closely cropped brown hair. Frank noticed that the man's handshake was firm and that there was concern in his deep green eyes.

Frank took a seat while Joe began admiring the many photographs of airplanes on the wall. One of the photos showed a handsome man in an air force uniform standing beside an F-16 fighter plane.

"That's my father," Jamal said with obvious pride. "He was a fighter pilot in the air force for twenty years."

"Ben Hawkins was one of the best flyboys in the force, I hear," McCafferty added.

"Ken was also a fighter jock in the force," Jamal said. "He came to work for my dad last year."

"I bet you weren't bad yourself," Frank said, recognizing McCafferty's "top-gun" confidence.

McCafferty shrugged. "I kept off the deck okay."

"What's it like flying a fighter jet?" Joe asked.

"What's it like?" McCafferty said. He seemed to search the air for an answer. "It's like nothing you've ever experienced. You transform into a bird for several hours. It's like . . . heaven."

"Makes me want to try it," Joe said.

"Same here," Frank agreed.

"Glad I've inspired you," McCafferty said, flashing a smile. "Now, if you guys will excuse me, I'm going to finish some tinkering I started on that Beechcraft. Holler if you need me, Jamal."

McCafferty gave a casual salute, then ambled out of the office.

"How did Tamara take the news?" Jamal asked the Hardys.

"Uh, listen, Jamal," Joe said, pulling off his coat, "there's something we need to tell you."

"Don't tell me you let me run that touchdown last Friday just to be polite?" Jamal joked.

"Afraid that's not it," Joe said with a smile. Taking a seat, he continued, "You already know our dad's a private detective. But the thing is, Frank and I are in the same business."

23

"You mean you help out your father?" Jamal asked.

"Sometimes we do," Joe said. "But we also investigate a lot of cases on our own. And we think your father's disappearance might be our next case."

Frank proceeded to give Jamal some background on their life as detectives. He also told him about their recent encounter with Tamara Fairbanks and her killer limo.

"Yeah," Joe joined in, "she's got a chauffeur with an attitude."

"So you believe," Jamal said after a long pause, "that someone may have tampered with my dad's plane because he wanted to kill Ian Fairbanks?"

"It's possible," Frank said. "And Tamara Fairbanks is already looking like a prime suspect."

"Can you think of anything that might be helpful to us?" Joe prompted. "Maybe something your father said about Ian Fairbanks."

"Before today," Jamal said, "my father never set eyes on Fairbanks. But while you guys were out, I was going through some things in my dad's desk, and I found this." Jamal picked up a small leather-bound notebook from the desk. "It's a journal my dad keeps."

"What about it?" Frank asked.

Jamal opened the notebook and found the page he wanted. "Check this out," Jamal said. He handed Frank the book and pointed to a handwritten passage. The entry Jamal indicated was dated just a few days earlier. Frank quickly scanned the page.

"It says here that Mr. Hawkins was getting 'bad vibes' about some regular client—a financial consultant named Dexter Cross."

"Why would your dad be so suspicious of a client?" Joe asked. He got up and read over his brother's shoulder. "'Bad vibes.' That's pretty vague."

"My dad had a problem with a smuggler using his airline recently," Jamal said. "It caused a lot of legal trouble for him, and it's made him extra cautious."

"Even if Cross is a smuggler," Frank said, "how would that tie him to Fairbanks's disappearance?"

"My dad did a little investigating on his own. He got some interesting information from a friend of his who works at Cross's bank. It's in the next entry."

Frank flipped to the next page, and he and Joe read the entry, hoping for concrete clues. "So Cross's checks were all coming from subsidiaries of the Fairbanks Corporation," Frank said.

"Hmm. The Fairbanks Corporation," Joe said eagerly. "Now we're getting somewhere."

"It doesn't necessarily mean anything," Frank cautioned his brother.

"But it might," Joe insisted. "Especially since the flight that disappeared just happened to be the one with Fairbanks on it."

"According to yesterday's entry," Jamal said,

"my dad was going to ask Mr. Fairbanks if he'd ever heard of this Cross guy. It's my dad's last entry in the book."

I sure hope it's not his last ever, Frank thought. He handed the journal back to Jamal.

"Okay," Joe said, trying to focus on the case. "What does this information tell us?"

"All we know for sure," Frank said, "is that Cross is getting payments from a division of the Fairbanks Corporation."

"Maybe Cross is working with Tamara Fairbanks on whatever her devious scheme is," Joe speculated. "Or maybe he was working with Ian Fairbanks in some capacity and things went sour. Apparently Ian Fairbanks makes enemies pretty fast."

"Both are possibilities," Frank stated. "But it's also possible that Cross's work for the Fairbanks Corporation, which is a very large organization, could be completely legitimate."

"Is there a file on Cross?" Joe asked.

"I already pulled it," Jamal said, lifting a manila folder off the desk.

"Let's see," Frank said, opening the folder and flipping through invoices. "Cross flew with Hawkins Air in February, April, June, August, and October of this year. That's every other month and always to different cities on the east coast. He's scheduled to fly to Washington, D.C., on December twentieth, which is tomorrow."

"McCafferty was his pilot for all the flights," Joe

said, looking over Frank's shoulder. "Did you ask him about Cross?"

"Sure did," Jamal replied. "Ken says Cross is pretty tight-lipped about his business dealings but is probably on the up and up."

"Cross's business address is 7684 Spring Street," Frank said, still examining the file. "That's a residential area. I guess Cross works out of his home. What do you say we drive out there and see if we can learn anything about the guy?"

"Up for it, Jamal?" Joe asked.

"I'm getting nervous just sitting around here," Jamal said. "Okay, guys. Let's go play detective."

The city of Bayport was now awash in a thick haze of falling snow. Frank had to pay careful attention to the road as he drove. Finally, the van came to the 7000 block of Spring Street, and he parked a few houses away from Cross's.

"Cross is either asleep or not home," Joe said, as they got out of the van and walked toward the dark town house.

"So you guys just go snooping around people's homes?" Jamal asked in amazement.

"We have been known to drop in uninvited from time to time," Joe said.

"Joe, you take that side," Frank said, pointing. "Jamal, come with me."

Frank and Jamal peered in every window on one side of the house while Joe took the other side. The lights were out, and the curtains were drawn, but with careful examination it was possible to pick out a few details. In less than five minutes the boys were heading back to the van.

"There wasn't much furniture," Frank said. "And there was a room that seemed like an office, but with no computer, no files, no fax—stuff you'd expect he'd have if he worked at home."

"In the bedroom, the closet door was open," Joe reported. "And I noticed there were only two suits in the closet. A financial consultant would have more than two suits, don't you think?"

"Jamal, notice anything weird?" Frank asked.

"Well, I saw a large tool bag on the kitchen floor," Jamal said. "Most people have some tools around, but this looked like a big collection. The kind a repairman or mechanic would have."

"You've got a good eye," Joe said.

The boys all got back in the van, with Joe at the wheel. Frank was glad to see their footprints to the house were being covered quickly by the snow. Soon there would be no visible trace of their mission.

"We didn't see anything highly unusual," Frank summed up. "Although there may have been things we missed. But we did see enough to make us wonder if Cross is really a financial consultant."

"So we have two suspects now," Joe declared. "Tamara Fairbanks and Dexter Cross."

"This is cool," Jamal said. "What's next?" Frank noticed that Jamal had more life in him now.

Taking an active role in the search for clues to his father's disappearance had improved his outlook.

Joe drove down a street lined with fast-food restaurants, their bright lights glowing against the dense fall of snow. "How about stopping for a burger?" he suggested.

"Good idea. Detective work makes me hungry," Jamal said.

"You sound like Chet." Joe grinned as he pulled into the parking lot of a burger joint. "Jamal, someday you have to meet our best buddy, Chet Morton."

As the boys downed cheeseburgers and fries, the Hardys entertained Jamal with some of their past adventures. Frank was glad he and Joe were able to keep Jamal's mind off his father's situation, at least for a while.

Soon Joe was back at the wheel of the van, driving through the snowy city. "I'm afraid there's not much more we can do tonight," Frank said. "But I think we should all meet at the hangar tomorrow and get a look at Mr. Cross in the flesh."

Frank saw the van was approaching a busy intersection. He was surprised that Joe wasn't slowing down. "Hey, Joe," Frank said, "that's a red light up there. Joe, did you hear me?"

"I heard you," Joe said, already applying pressure to the brake pedal. "But I can't slow down."

"What do you mean?" Frank asked, seeing the alarmed look on Joe's face.

"I mean the brakes aren't working." Joe shoved his foot down hard on the brake pedal. "The emergency brake's not working either," he said as he yanked the lever several times. "Can I turn somewhere?"

"No," Jamal said, glancing quickly around. "There are cars in the lane to the right, and more coming from the other direction."

"The light just changed to yellow," Frank added gravely.

Gripping the steering wheel, Joe could see cars passing through the intersection ahead. Then the light changed to red, and the cars stopped to let traffic from the cross street go through. The van wasn't going very fast, but it wasn't stopping either. And it was rapidly approaching the car directly in front of it, which was coming to a stop for the red light.

"Honk the horn!" Frank urged.

Joe pushed down on the horn to send out a loud warning that he couldn't stop. The car ahead swerved into the right hand lane, giving Joe a bit more breathing room.

But then the van's horn was answered by a much louder, deeper-toned horn. With a jolt to his system, Joe saw it—a giant Mack truck barreling for the intersection from the cross street. The truck was on a direct collision course with the van!

4 The Secret of the Birds

Through the swirling snow, Joe could see the monstrous truck plowing across the intersection ahead. The deep sound of its horn blared nightmarishly loud, and it seemed to Joe as if time stood still.

"Cars still to my right?" Joe called desperately.

"Yeah," Jamal called back.

"Joe, you've got five seconds," Frank warned.

"Hang on!" Joe called.

Joe swung the wheel hard to the left, and the van swerved wildly into the opposite lane—skidding and sliding—then it jumped the curb and crashed violently into the trunk of a tree. Joe braced himself against the steering wheel, but his seatbelt stopped him from being thrown forward. Twenty feet ahead, the truck roared by, the sound of its horn fading in the distance.

Joe, Frank, and Jamal sat in the van, dazed. Soon Joe became aware of the van's engine sputtering into silence.

"Everyone okay?" Joe asked finally.

"I'm still in one piece," Frank answered.

"Me, too," Jamal said. "Nice save, Joseph."

The boys unstrapped their seat belts and climbed unsteadily out of the van. Several cars had stopped to see if they needed help, but Frank waved them on.

"The van took a pretty nasty hit," Joe said, seeing that the front of the van had crumpled against the tree trunk like a soda can. "I'm afraid it's out of commission."

"So, uh, listen, guys," Jamal said, rubbing the back of his neck. "When was the last time you guys had your brakes checked?"

"I guess it's been a while," Frank answered. "And this snow sure doesn't help any. But . . ."

"But what?" Jamal persisted. "I always check out a plane before I fly it."

"I'm sure you do," Joe said, a little irritated. "But maybe somebody *fixed* those brakes not to work."

"Somebody could have emptied the brake fluid while we were in the burger place," Frank guessed. "In this weather, who would notice?"

"Hold it," Jamal said. "Somebody who?"

"Somebody who doesn't want us on the case," Joe pointed out. "Maybe that chauffeur has been following us tonight. Or maybe Dexter Cross saw us at his place somehow. That tool bag in his kitchen might mean he'd have the know-how."

"There's a pay phone up the block," Frank said. "Let's call Chet to get us. Then we'll have to call a tow truck."

The boys began trudging through the snow. "Wow!" Jamal exclaimed. "I didn't realize this detective business was so dangerous."

"This is nothing," Joe said. "We're just getting warmed up."

It was still cold the following morning, but the sky was bright and clear. Just after seven, Jamal picked up the Hardys in his car and drove toward the airport. There was still no word on Mr. Hawkins or his plane, and Jamal looked as if he had barely slept.

"I called Con Riley last night," Frank informed Jamal. "That's our friend on the police force. I told him what we'd learned about Tamara Fairbanks and Dexter Cross. He said he would pass on the info to the detective handling the case."

"Riley said the FBI is also interested," Joe added. "Apparently everybody suspects somebody was out to get Ian Fairbanks."

"Bad luck for my dad," Jamal said quietly.

Within thirty minutes Jamal was driving along

the airport tarmac. Joe noticed a number of trucks plowing last night's snow from the runways. As Jamal pulled up in front of the Hawkins Air Service hangar, Joe saw Ken McCafferty checking over a lightplane that had HAS lettered on the side.

"Morning," McCafferty called as the boys stepped out of the car. "Betty told me there's still no news about your dad, Jamal. I'm real sorry, kid."

"Thanks," Jamal said.

"Hang in there," McCafferty encouraged. "If anyone has a chance of surviving this thing, it's Ben Hawkins. He's one of the toughest guys I know."

Jamal led the Hardys into the hangar, where they found Betty at her desk. "I just spoke to the Civil Air Patrol," Betty reported. "They've been flying over the mountains all night, and they sent out a bunch of new planes at dawn. The problem is, there was a big snowfall in the Adirondacks last night that's making the search more difficult."

"Thanks for the update," Jamal said.

"Oh, Frank, Joe, how did it go with Tamara Fairbanks?" Betty asked, picking up a stapler.

"It went okay," Frank said, thinking it would be best to keep the details to himself.

"I just love that lady," Betty said, trying to pull open the stapler. "She's everything I'd like to be. Rich, intelligent, a fabulous dresser."

"Have you met her?" Joe asked.

"Just once," Betty answered. "This guy I used to date—Sammy—used to be her chauffeur. But then she fired him. She said she was expecting some trouble and needed someone who could be a chauffeur *and* a bodyguard. Now she's got some guy who looks like Frankenstein.''

"He acts like it, too,'' Joe grumbled.

"Cross should be here soon,'' Frank said, checking his watch. "You guys better disappear.''

"Right,'' Joe said. He and Jamal split for Mr. Hawkins's office. The plan was for Joe and Jamal to lay low when Cross arrived, in case they needed to follow the man at some future point. This way Cross would only have seen Frank.

Betty began banging the stapler on the desk.

"What does Sammy do now?'' Frank asked her.

"He drives a cab in the line out here at the airport,'' Betty said. "He works the night shift, though, so fortunately I never run into him.''

A few minutes later, a well-dressed man of about forty strolled into the hangar. He wore tortoiseshell glasses and carried an expensive leather briefcase.

"Good morning, Mr. Cross,'' Betty said, dropping the stapler to adjust her hair. "Would you like some coffee?''

"Black, please,'' Dexter Cross said. He took a seat and pulled a newspaper from his trenchcoat.

"Coming up.'' Betty smiled, heading for the coffee machine across the hangar.

Cross began reading his newspaper. Frank could see the front page headline, which read, "Millionaire Tycoon Ian Fairbanks Missing!''

Frank sat on the metal chair next to Cross. "Where you flying to?" he inquired casually.

"Washington, D.C.," Cross answered, not bothering to look up from his newspaper.

"Business?" Frank asked.

"That's right," Cross said.

"What sort of work do you do?" Frank asked.

"Consulting," Cross said, still reading the paper.

"What sort of consulting?" Frank persisted.

"Financial," Cross replied.

"You know, I'm curious," Frank kept on. "What exactly does a financial consultant do? I've always wondered."

Cross looked up from his paper and adjusted his glasses. Frank thought he seemed nervous.

"Financial consulting," Cross answered, "encompasses a wide variety of things. Excuse me."

Cross got up and went into the men's room. Frank glanced around and saw that Betty was still at the coffee machine. On an impulse, he pulled a metal pick from his pocket and knelt down by Cross's briefcase. With a deft turn of the pick, Frank opened the case.

The briefcase was absolutely empty!

Interesting, Frank thought. He quickly closed the case and relocked it. Then he hurried into Mr. Hawkins's office and pulled the door shut behind him.

"If Cross knows anything about financial consulting, he sure didn't want to share it with me," Frank whispered to Joe and Jamal. "And, listen. I picked open his briefcase and there wasn't a single thing inside it. Nothing. This guy is a phony if you ask me. Jamal, is it possible to get a plane and follow Cross to D.C. so we can see for ourselves what he's doing there?"

"Anything to help find my dad," Jamal said. "All I've got to do is give Betty a flight plan to file."

"I just called the auto shop," Joe told Frank. "The van will be ready in three days. They also said there were two punctures on the brake line and a cut cable on the emergency brake. In other words, that accident last night was no accident."

Ten minutes later McCafferty and Cross took off in the lightplane McCafferty had been checking. As soon as they left, Jamal did a preflight check on a Cessna Cardinal that also had HAS stenciled on the side.

Jamal and the Hardys climbed inside the Cessna's small four-seat cabin. Jamal and Frank sat up front, Joe in back. As the boys all put on headsets and strapped in, Frank noticed the instrument panel on the Cessna was much more rudimentary than that of the simulated 727.

"Clear!" Jamal yelled out the window from the pilot seat. Then he turned the ignition key, and the Cessna's propeller swirled to life.

"Bayport ground control," Jamal said into his headset mike, "this is Cessna two-five-four-tango at Hawkins hangar. Ready to taxi to the active runway."

"Morning, Jamal," a voice crackled over all three

headsets. "Skies are clear for VFR, and you are clear to taxi to runway four."

Frank knew that VFR stood for visual flight rules, meaning that the pilot had to fly where he could see the ground at all times.

As the engine grew louder, Jamal guided the Cessna onto runway four and tuned into a new radio frequency. "Bayport tower," Jamal said. "Cessna two-five-four-tango is at runway four and I am requesting clearance for takeoff."

"Cessna two-five," the tower voice replied, "you are cleared for takeoff, sir."

Jamal pushed in the throttle knob, the engine roared louder, and the plane began rolling down the runway. As the Cessna picked up speed, Jamal eased back on the control wheel, and the little white plane lifted gracefully into the sky.

"Nice take-off," Frank said with admiration.

"Experience helps," Jamal said. "My dad started giving me lessons when I was seven."

As the Cessna continued angling upward, the Hardys watched the airport and buildings and homes of Bayport grow smaller and smaller beneath them.

"Okay, back there, Joseph?" Jamal asked. "Wouldn't want you getting airsick."

"Ha ha," Joe said. "You know, I just don't understand how these things stay up in the air."

"It's the secret of the birds," Jamal said, watching the altimeter dial. "We've learned to copy a few of their techniques pretty well, but we'll never be able to master flight the way they do."

The plane kept climbing upward. Soon white, vaporous clouds were visible out the windows.

"I'll catch a better tailwind above the clouds," Jamal explained. "That way I'll be sure to beat Cross to D.C. so we can pick up his trail from the airport. Meanwhile, Hardy bros, tell me about some more of your famous cases."

As Jamal expertly guided the Cessna on a southwesterly course, Frank and Joe related a few of their favorite cases. In less than three hours, Jamal began descending through the clouds, and the boys caught a bird's-eye view of Washington, D.C.

"I'd like to thank you for flying Hawkins Air," Jamal announced in a mock pilot's voice. "And welcome to our nation's capital."

Jamal landed the plane at an auxiliary airport on the outskirts of D.C. He had brought a tarp along, and the Hardys helped him cover the plane with it so Dexter Cross wouldn't recognize the HAS logo if his plane happened to be parked nearby.

Next Jamal and the Hardys rented a car and waited inside it in front of the main airport building. Within half an hour, they saw Dexter Cross step out of the building.

"Here he comes," Joe said. "Where's McCafferty?"

"He'll probably hang out at the airport awhile and swap pilot stories," Jamal answered.

Cross climbed in a taxi and drove away. "Okay, let's see what Mr. Cross is up to," Frank said. He began following the taxi in the rental car.

The traffic leading into D.C. was extremely thick, but Frank managed to tail the taxi into the city and along the grassy mall they had glimpsed from the air. Frank stopped a safe distance away when the taxi let Cross off at an impressive building made of glass and concrete.

"It's the Smithsonian Air and Space Museum," Jamal pointed out. "Awesome place."

"I'm going after him," Joe said, opening the car door. "After you guys park, come inside."

Joe followed Cross through the museum's front entrance. All around, airplanes hung suspended from the ceiling. Joe saw that there were enough visitors milling about to give him plenty of cover.

Cross stopped to look up at a crude airplane made mostly of long fabric wings. Joe realized it was the Wright Brothers' *Flyer*, the plane that in 1903 made the first powered flight through the air.

Cross continued past the entrance area and began walking under a collection of open-cockpit airplanes from the 1920s and '30s. Joe followed, wondering what Cross was doing here. Was he meeting someone? He couldn't have chartered a flight to Washington, D.C., just to look at famous airplanes.

Next, Cross walked up a staircase to the second floor of the museum, and Joe followed him into an exhibit room, keeping a careful distance.

The room was devoted to fighter planes from World War I. When Joe saw him, Cross was looking at an American biplane that hung suspended against a dramatic backdrop of a stormy sky.

Joe pretended to be studying a German biplane with a mannequin pilot in the cockpit. He stole a quick glance at Cross, who at that exact moment turned and looked at Joe. Joe quickly looked away.

When Joe turned back around, he caught a glimpse of Cross's trenchcoat leaving the room.

Maybe he knows I'm following him, Joe thought as he hurried back into the hallway and saw Cross going into another exhibit room. Deciding to risk it, Joe ducked in after him.

The entire room was a replica of the planet Mars. Through a hazy light, Joe could see salmon-colored rocks and crags and caves. But he saw no sign of Cross. Joe moved quickly through the eerie Martian landscape, passing astronauts and robots and curious tourists, until he found himself back in a museum hallway. Weird, Joe thought. For a financial consultant, Cross had just pulled off a pretty slick disappearing act.

To Joe's left was a black Mercury space capsule, the one that first carried a U.S. astronaut into orbit. To Joe's right was a balcony overlooking a back entrance of the ground floor.

A small boy was perched on the balcony's metal railing. Dangerous place to sit, Joe thought as his eyes searched for a glimpse of Cross.

Suddenly Dexter Cross sprung out from behind

41

the capsule and grabbed Joe by the shirt. "Stop following me," Cross snarled, "or I'll send you to the moon!"

Cross gave Joe a rough shove and stalked away. Joe staggered back a few steps, then felt his body hit something. Then that something let out a terrified screech.

Joe whipped around to see the kid on the balcony tumbling backward into empty space!

5 The Force

Instantly Joe's arms shot out, desperately reaching for the boy, but all he grabbed was air.

"Help!" the boy screamed. Luckily, the boy grabbed onto a jutting ledge on the other side of the railing. He was dangling from the ledge with two hands. Joe knew he couldn't hold on for long.

"Help me!" the boy cried frantically.

"I will," Joe said, leaning over the balcony. He scanned the area, but they were by a back entrance and the hallway was empty.

"Help!" the boy pleaded again. "I'm slipping!"

Joe hoisted himself onto the railing and stretched out to reach the boy. Rats! Joe thought. He was just a few inches short of where the boy hung.

"Hang on," Joe urged. "Just a minute longer."

"I caaaan't!" the boy cried.

Joe watched in horror as the boy's fingers slipped off the ledge! He felt as if his stomach had just plummeted down into his feet as he watched the boy drop.

Just then a figure dashed under the balcony. Joe saw the boy fall right into Jamal's extended arms.

"Gotcha!" Jamal exclaimed.

"Jamal," Joe gasped.

"I heard someone screaming," Jamal called to Joe as he gently set the boy down. "I thought you'd gotten yourself into another mess, but I guess it was just this kid you threw off the balcony."

"Yeah, it's my new hobby," Joe called back. "Kid-tossing. Next time he should use a bungee cord. Take care of him while I go after Cross!"

Joe raced to a spot on the balcony where he could look down at the main area of the ground floor. Soon he saw Cross in the crowd, heading toward an exit at the far end of the museum. Scanning the ground floor, Joe spotted Frank near the museum's front entrance.

"Frank!" Joe yelled down. Frank looked up and saw Joe, who was pointing in the direction Cross was headed. Without missing a beat, Frank began running after Cross. Joe watched Cross, then Frank, rush out of the museum.

Ten minutes later Frank met up with Joe and Jamal underneath the *Spirit of St. Louis*, the tarnished silver airplane in which Charles Lindbergh had made the first crossing of the Atlantic Ocean.

44

"By the time I got outside, he was gone," Frank explained. "He probably caught a cab. Sorry."

"What was he doing here?" Joe wondered.

"Beats me," Jamal said. "But he must have other business in town, because he booked his plane for overnight."

"I'm afraid we've lost his trail," Frank said.

"Well, should we get some lunch and head back to Bayport?" Joe asked.

"Actually," Jamal said, "I thought of something else I'd like to do while we're in the area. There's a general at Andrews Air Force Base who was in flight training with my dad. They were pretty tight back then, and they stay in touch. Maybe he can pull some strings and get some more people searching for my dad's plane."

"Nothing like a general for pulling strings," Frank commented. "Let's go to the base."

After a quick lunch at the museum, Jamal and the Hardys were on the road. Before long, they drove through the main gate of Andrews Air Force Base, in nearby Virginia.

Frank parked the car, and Jamal ran up to a guard station near the gate. Waiting in the car, all the Hardys could see was a concrete road densely lined with trees. It looked more like a suburban neighborhood than an air force base, Frank thought. A few minutes later, Jamal returned.

"They put in a call to the general," Jamal explained. "He said he'd be here in fifteen minutes."

Exactly fifteen minutes later, a car drove up. A

man with gray hair and a dark blue air force uniform stepped out. "You must be Ben's boy," the man told Jamal. "I'm General Tom Radman."

Joe noticed three stars on the epaulets of the general's crisp uniform. He could tell this was a man who got things done.

"I'm Jamal, sir," Jamal said. "And these are my friends Frank and Joe Hardy."

"Why don't you boys jump in my car?" the general suggested after shaking everyone's hand.

As the general drove the boys through the base, Jamal explained about Mr. Hawkins's missing plane. After a few minutes, the general parked in front of a small redbrick building. "This is the flight planning center," General Radman announced. "Let's go inside and see what I can do for my old buddy Ben Hawkins."

The boys followed the general into a large room with maps and charts on every wall. "First, let's get a progress report from the Civil Air Patrol," the general said, picking up a phone.

"What exactly is the Civil Air Patrol?" Joe asked Jamal as the general spoke into the phone.

"When a plane is missing," Jamal explained, "they're usually the ones that go searching for it. By air and sometimes by land. It's a volunteer organization, but they often work with the air force. And a lot of the volunteers are kids."

"Can anyone join?" Frank asked.

"Anyone over twelve," Jamal answered.

The general made another call, then hung up the

phone. He pulled out a detailed map of New York state and laid it on a large table.

"The radar first lost contact with Mr. Hawkins right here," the general said, pointing to a spot on the map. "So the plane is bound to be somewhere in this area," he said, sweeping his hand over the map. "But it's a big area we're talking about, and those mountains are buried under a lot of snow right now."

"And it's cold there," Jamal said softly.

"However," the general continued, "I just called the commanding officer out at Plattsburgh Air Force Base in upstate New York. He's going to send two dozen more planes out, and with the extra people, we've got a much better chance of finding Ben. Jamal, I promise the force will do everything within its power to bring your dad home."

"I appreciate the effort," Jamal said. Joe thought his friend seemed to be searching for his father in the colored mountains of the map.

"Did Jamal say you boys were detectives?" the general said, turning to the Hardys.

"Yes, he did," Frank confirmed.

"Well, I think that's just great," the general said, eyeing the two Hardys. "Big organizations like the military and the police are absolutely essential. But sometimes I bet a couple of smart kids can get the job done better than any of them."

"We try," Joe said. Frank grinned at his brother's unaccustomed modesty.

"Why don't we step outside," the general said,

putting a fatherly arm around Jamal. "I'll show you the type of jet Mr. Hawkins flew for the force."

General Radman led the boys outside and past the domed hangars. On a nearby runway, six dark gray fighter jets were lined up in takeoff formation.

"Those are F-16 fighter jets," the general explained. "Also known as Fighting Falcons. The Falcon is one of the most sophisticated fighter planes in the world."

"Where are they going?" Frank asked.

"Practice maneuvers," the general said. "They'll dogfight each other over New Jersey today."

Just then two of the gray F-16s began racing side by side down the runway, their jet engines roaring in the distance. The two fighters lifted off the ground in perfect unison, and seconds later they disappeared into the sky.

"My dad loved flying the Falcon," Jamal said with pride. "Ken McCafferty flew them, too."

"They're painted that color gray," the general said, "to make them almost invisible in the sky."

"How fast can they go?" Frank asked.

"Supersonic," the general said. "They have a maximum flying speed of Mach 2. That's twice the speed of sound."

A moment later two more F-16s roared down the runway in tandem. Together they lifted into the air, soon disappearing from view.

"What about the rumors that the air force has a hypersonic plane?" Jamal asked the general.

The general smiled, his eyes still on the sky.

"Hypersonic?" Joe asked. "I don't know what that means."

"It means a flying speed of at least Mach 5.4," Jamal explained. "That's over five times the speed of sound."

"Wow!" Joe exclaimed. Frank let out a low whistle.

"Out in Nevada," Jamal continued, "the air force has a supersecret base known as Dreamland. There's a rumor that a top secret hypersonic plane is being tested out there."

"Are the rumors true?" Joe asked the general.

"People say we've got flying saucers out there, too," the general said, still watching the sky. "Don't believe everything you hear, son."

"Yes, sir," Joe replied as the last two F-16s roared down the runway and vanished into the sky.

It was around dusk when Jamal and the Hardys returned to the D.C. airport. After they dropped off the rental car, the boys walked across the tarmac toward their plane. Frank was surprised to see that McCafferty's plane was gone, since Cross had been booked overnight, but Jamal figured Ken took the plane out for some recreational flying.

After the boys pulled the tarp off the Cessna, Jamal carefully checked the airplane again. When he decided all systems were go, the boys climbed inside the plane, strapped in, and took off again.

Jamal put the plane into a banking turn over the city. "The weather service said a cold front was coming down from Canada," Jamal explained. "It may bring some snow, so I'm taking us over the ocean to avoid it. Frank, do you know how to chart a course?"

"Sure do," Frank said, picking up a folded map.

"Why don't you keep track of our position," Jamal suggested. "Always a good idea over water."

"You got it," Frank said as he glanced out the window. He began drawing a line on the map with a pen, approximating the airplane's course.

An hour later the plane was flying over the Atlantic Ocean. As the sun sank on the western horizon, Joe looked down at the endless expanse of water stretched out below.

"Hang on," Jamal warned. He pushed down the control wheel, swooping and circling the plane in a fancy aerobatic maneuver.

Joe felt the world turn upside down and sideways and right side up again. "What are you doing?" he called from the backseat, his stomach feeling every move the plane made.

"I'm writing a *J*," Jamal replied. "I guess you could call it my flying signature." Jamal finished the maneuver and brought the plane back to a level position.

"Hey, Jamal," Joe joked, "where's the barf bag?"

Suddenly a sputtering sound came from the front of the Cessna.

"What's that?" Frank asked, a little concerned.

"Sounds like some ice is forming in the carburetor," Jamal said, pulling out a knob on the instrument panel. "It's a common problem in colder weather. I've turned the carb-heat on, and it should melt the ice any minute now."

As the sun sank deeper, night began spreading its shadow across the vast Atlantic. Jamal pushed a button, and instantly the dials glowed from the instrument panel.

"Do you find it harder flying in the dark?" Frank asked, making a notation on the chart.

"That's one advantage we have over the birds," Jamal said. "Birds can fly only if they can see where they're going. But if a pilot knows his instrument panel, he can fly just fine in the dark."

All around the airplane, the ocean and sky had merged into one vast canvas of blackness. For a long while the boys said nothing. They just felt the night's presence and listened to the steady drone of the Cessna's engine.

"Peaceful up here, isn't it?" Jamal said.

"Yeah, it really—" Joe began. He was interrupted by the sputtering engine.

"Uh-oh," Frank said. "The carb-heat still isn't working."

Jamal's expression was calm as he fiddled with the carb-heat knob, but Frank could see fear etched on his Jamal's face.

The engine sputtered again. And again.

"Not that I'm worried or anything," Joe said, trying to act casual. "But, uh, what happens if the carb-heat is broken? I mean, is that really bad?"

He had complete faith in Jamal's piloting skill, but his friend's next words made Joe's heart stop.

"Guys," Jamal said, his voice now trembling, "I think the ice is about to kill our engine. The plane is going down."

6 Dead Reckoning

"How much time have we got?" Frank asked urgently.

"We've got maybe ten minutes to fly," Jamal responded, suddenly banking the plane into a turn.

"We better head back for land," Joe advised.

"I'm already doing that," Jamal said, eyes on the instrument panel. "But we're at least fifty miles out over the ocean. I doubt we'll make it back to shore."

Frank swallowed hard. "What are you saying? That we have to ditch it in the ocean?"

"That's right," Jamal said, flipping a switch. "I'm turning on the landing lights. Joe, check for signs of a boat or even a buoy."

As he looked out the window, Joe saw a circle of light illuminating the ocean. The water below was dark and rolling and endless. Joe took a breath. He couldn't even imagine being stranded down there.

"I don't see anything but ocean," Joe said. "It's going to be tough for someone to find us."

The engine coughed several times, roughly bumping the plane up and down each time.

"Remember," Jamal urged, "the most important thing in a flight crisis is to stay cool."

"You're right," Frank said, taking a deep breath. "Tell us what to do, pal. It's your plane."

"Joe, keep looking for a marker," Jamal instructed. "Frank, tune in to frequency 123.8. It's the nearest enroute control center. I'll fly and you explain our situation to the controller."

Frank turned the radio knobs until the digital numbers showed 123.8. Immediately static came crackling through all three headsets.

"Come in," Frank spoke into his headset. "This is Cessna two-five-four-tango. Do you read me?"

A few tense moments went by. Frank and Joe exchanged a glance. Then a male voice crackled over the radio. "Cessna two-five, this is your enroute control. Go ahead, sir."

"We are in a Cessna Cardinal flying over the Atlantic Ocean," Frank explained, trying to keep his voice steady. "We're about fifty miles off the coast of Delaware. We have ice cutting off our fuel supply and our carb-heat isn't working. We are heading for land, but we don't expect to make it."

"Is the pilot declaring an emergency?" the voice asked.

"Yes, he is," Jamal answered.

"All right," the voice said in a soothing tone. "My name is Jim, and I'm going to help you. Give me a second while I alert the Coast Guard Rescue Center."

Frank realized their lives were now in the hands of Jim—a stranger sitting in a room somewhere miles away who was nothing more than a voice in a headset.

"Cessna two-five," Jim finally came back. "I've alerted the Coast Guard. Now, for them to find you, we need to get a decent bearing on your location."

"Are you reading us on radar?" Jamal asked.

"Unfortunately, no," Jim said. "You're too far out in the water for my radar to pick you up. Which also means we won't be able to triangulate your position. And your ELT may not go off once it hits the water. Have you spotted any boats or markers out there?"

"Nothing," Joe said over the sound of the coughing engine. Then he turned back to the window. The ocean looked darker and colder every minute.

"Okay," Jim continued. "Let's try to find your position by dead reckoning."

"I don't like the sound of that," Joe muttered. "What does 'dead reckoning' mean?"

"It means we estimate your location through course, speed, time, and wind," Jim explained. "What is the last landmark you noticed on the flight?"

"At approximately seventeen hundred," Frank

said, glancing at his chart, "we passed over the town of Ridge Harbor."

"What has been your course since then?" Jim asked.

"We flew on a heading of sixty degrees east for about twenty miles," Frank said, following the lines he had drawn on the chart. "Then we turned north and flew on a heading of thirty degrees for about, oh, forty miles."

"And what has your airspeed been?" Jim asked.

"Approximately one hundred twenty knots," Frank said, glancing at the airspeed dial.

"Good navigating," Jim said. "Now I'm calculating your position against the current wind conditions to get a rough idea of where you are. However, it's just a rough idea. It may take some time for the Coast Guard to find you down there."

"We don't have any time," Frank said, glancing at the dark waves. "The plane won't float for long, and the water will be close to freezing."

"I know," Jim said. "You may have to pretend you're polar bears for a few minutes."

Beneath the humor, Frank could hear a tinge of deep concern in Jim's voice. Suddenly Frank felt a kinship with this kind voice located many miles away.

The engine started coughing as though it had a bad case of the flu, the plane jolting roughly each time.

"We can't stay airborne much longer," Jamal

said, easing the control wheel forward. "I'm going to land while I still have some control. Joe, there's a box of flares and a gun in the back. Get them, please. Unfortunately we don't have a flotation device."

"Roger," Joe said, already opening the metal box.

Looking out the window, Frank saw the plane angling toward the ominous waves of the ocean.

"Jim, we're going in," Frank said. "We'll be losing contact with you any second so, uh, thanks a million for all your help."

"You can buy me a box of cigars when you get back," Jim said. "By the way, what are your names?"

Frank knew why Jim was asking this question. It was in case their bodies were lost at sea.

"I'm Frank Hardy," Frank said. "I'm here with my brother, Joe Hardy, and our good friend Jamal Hawkins."

"Stay brave, boys," Jim encouraged. "We are going to find you. Good luck."

"This is it," Jamal warned, guiding the control wheel. "Frank, crack your door so we don't get trapped." Frank turned the latch and opened his door slightly. Seconds later, the Cessna bounced on the water like a skipping rock, then it plopped to a sudden halt. The engine conked into silence.

"Abandon ship," Jamal called.

The boys climbed quickly through Frank's door,

then hoisted themselves onto the top of the plane. The plane was rocking on the choppy waves, making the task tricky, but soon all three boys were sitting astride the floating Cessna. Frank shut the door with his leg to keep water from seeping into the plane.

"Let's just ride it like it was a horse," Jamal suggested. "It'll be the best way to stay on."

"I agree," Frank said with a shiver. He was suddenly aware of how cold it was. And he knew the water would be even colder.

"I'll shoot a flare," Joe said, pulling a flare and flare gun from his coat. Joe loaded it and fired. The flare whistled high into the sky, exploding in a brilliant flash of red.

Joe looked around. A nearly full moon shone faintly through the clouds, illuminating the infinite Atlantic Ocean surrounding them. As the plane rocked back and forth in the waves, Joe swallowed hard, trying to swallow his fear.

"Okay," Frank said. "Let's talk about something to keep our minds off the water."

"Let's talk about my plane," Jamal said angrily. "Someone must have tampered with the cable on the carb-heat control and was careful to do it in a way I wouldn't notice in the pre-takeoff check. And you know what? Whoever it was meant for us to die tonight."

"It's probably the same party responsible for fixing our brakes last night," Frank added. "And it's probably the same party responsible for downing the plane with Ian Fairbanks."

"We must know something this person doesn't want us to know," Joe figured. "But what?" Joe stole a glance at the rolling waves. He was instantly sorry.

"Stay on the case," Frank warned, seeing the look on his brother's face.

"Dexter Cross knows we're suspicious of him," Jamal said, "and apparently Tamara Fairbanks is also nervous about you guys. But we don't know why."

"Okay, let's try working another way," Frank suggested. "Who could have made those accidents happen?"

"Supposedly Fairbanks was traveling incognito to Ottawa," Joe pointed out. "And we made the decision to fly to D.C. on the spur of the moment. So who could have known about those two flights?"

"Every time a Hawkins plane goes up," Jamal explained, "Betty files a flight plan with the flight station. But that's not really public information. Besides, only the pilot's name is listed."

"Remember, Cross saw me at the museum," Joe said. "Maybe he somehow connected me to Hawkins Air. He had time to get to the D.C. airport and sabotage our plane before we got back to it. And if he's been dealing with Fairbanks, he may have known about the Fairbanks flight, too."

"And don't forget that tool bag in his kitchen,"

59

Jamal added. "Maybe he knows something about aircraft mechanics."

"Chauffeurs often know something about engines," Joe said. "Let's not forget Frankenstein, Tamara's driver. But how would he know about the flights?"

"What about Ken McCafferty?" Frank said, after a moment. "He could have known about the Fairbanks flight, and he also could have spotted our plane in D.C."

"Ken is awfully good with aircraft repair," Jamal added. "He's always tinkering with Dad's planes. But is Ken really a suspect?"

"Should he be?" Joe asked. "You know the guy."

"Yeah, I do know him," Jamal said thoughtfully. "Ken's one of the nicest guys I know."

Suddenly Frank felt water lapping at his sneakers. While the boys avoided thinking about the water, the plane had been steadily sinking, and the Cessna was now more than halfway down. Frank realized they had maybe five minutes to stay afloat.

"Agggh." Joe winced as water crept into his sock. It was icy cold.

"Don't think about it," Frank urged.

"Hard not to," Joe snapped. "It's everywhere."

"Shhh," Frank whispered. "Listen."

The three boys listened intently, and sure enough they heard a dim buzz in the distance.

"Is that my imagination or is that the beautiful sound of a helicopter?" Jamal asked.

"I hear it, too," Joe said, pulling another flare from his coat. His hands were stiff and shaky from the cold, but he managed to load the gun and shoot it, sending the flare whistling overhead. Frank had brought a flashlight and began blinking its beam on and off.

The distant buzz grew louder and louder, and the boys searched the black sky for a light.

Jamal was the first to spot it. "It's the rescue copter!" he shrieked at the top of his lungs. "Over here!" he cried, waving an arm.

"Hooray!" Joe cheered.

Frank joined in as loud as he could. They knew they would be spotted by the copter, but they yelled till they were hoarse, anyway. They were still alive, and they'd been saved!

It wasn't long before the helicopter approached and whirled noisily over the boys. A bright searchlight beamed down from the copter, scanned the water, then landed directly on Frank, Joe, and Jamal.

In the beam of the copter's light, the boys saw a rescue harness being lowered down to them. "Ride the harness up one at a time!" a megaphoned-voice boomed down from the copter.

"After you, Joe," Frank said, grabbing the harness.

"Thanks," Joe said, taking a seat on the device.

Riding the harness as if it were a swing, Joe was lifted quickly upward toward the whirling helicopter. When the harness reached the copter, Joe was hauled into the cabin by two Coast Guard men in orange flight suits.

Within minutes Frank and Jamal were also safely inside the copter. Each boy was given a thick blanket to wrap around himself and a cup of hot tea.

"Which one of you is Jamal Hawkins?" one of the Coast Guard men asked when the boys were settled.

"That's me," Jamal said, lowering his cup.

"General Radman heard your name on the emergency squawk and told us to give you a message," the man said. "It's about your father. An hour ago the air force found his plane in the Adirondack mountains. Your father was banged up some and was suffering a bit from hypothermia, but he's basically okay."

Jamal closed his eyes tight a moment. When he opened them, Joe could see joy rushing into his friend's face.

"Yes, yes, yes!" Jamal shouted in triumph.

Frank gave Jamal's arm a squeeze, and Joe slapped Jamal's knee. The good news warmed Frank and Joe far more than the steaming hot tea.

"Mr. Hawkins is now resting comfortably at the Plattsburgh Air Force Base hospital," the Coast Guard man continued.

"What about the passenger on his plane?" Frank asked. "Ian Fairbanks. Is he okay?"

"That's the mysterious part," the Coast Guard man answered. "Fairbanks wasn't on the plane when it was found, and not even Mr. Hawkins knows where he is. Search teams are combing the area for him by air and ground. It's like the man just disappeared."

7 Survivor

Ten minutes later the copter landed at a Coast Guard base off the Delaware shore. General Radman had arranged for Jamal to be driven to nearby Dover Air Force Base. From there Jamal would fly to the Plattsburgh Air Force Base in upstate New York to see his father. Joe decided to tag along and get some firsthand information from Mr. Hawkins.

Frank planned to travel immediately back to Bayport in the hope that he might pick up some new leads. Not wanting to take any more chances after the day's nearly fatal flight, Frank announced he would be going home by train. "I've had enough adventure for one day," he grumbled.

"Yeah," Joe agreed. "Maybe we should take a hydroplane this time, Jamal, just to be on the safe side."

It was eleven o'clock at night when Jamal and Joe entered the dimly lit hospital room in Plattsburgh where Mr. Hawkins lay sleeping. The man's face was bandaged, and he had a cast on one arm and an IV tube running into his other arm. Jamal looked at his father for a long moment.

After several minutes Mr. Hawkins opened his eyes. "Hey, buddy," he said slowly. "Good to see you."

"Good to see you too, Dad," Jamal said. He touched his father gently on the shoulder. "This is my friend Joe Hardy. He's been wanting to meet you."

"Hi, Joe," Mr. Hawkins said, managing a smile.

"Hi, Mr. Hawkins," Joe said, smiling back.

"I guess you boys are wondering what happened to my plane," Mr. Hawkins said, sitting up in the bed.

"We can talk about it later," Jamal said.

"No, let's talk about it now," Mr. Hawkins said, shifting to get more comfortable. "Maybe you boys can help me figure things out."

"Maybe we can," Joe said. He and Jamal pulled up chairs near the bed to hear Mr. Hawkins's story. Joe pulled out a pen and memo pad for notes.

"When I checked the plane before takeoff in Ottawa," Mr. Hawkins began, "everything seemed to be just fine. So Fairbanks and I took off for the return journey. Shortly after we crossed into New York State, I heard two small explosions. One in the front of the plane, the other in the rear. The explosions weren't big enough to destroy the plane, but the front one killed the engine. Right away we started losing airspeed."

"What did Fairbanks do?" Joe asked.

"He grabbed a parachute pack he had brought along," Mr. Hawkins said. "When he boarded he told me he always flew with a parachute because he was afraid of attempts on his life. At the time, I thought he was just being paranoid. . . ." Mr. Hawkins paused for a moment, then shook his head. "Maybe he had a right to be."

"Meanwhile you were struggling to control the plane, I bet," Jamal said.

"I knew the plane was going down," Mr. Hawkins said, "but I was trying to make it a controlled crash. The plane started bucking pretty bad and I guess I hit my head, because I was knocked out for a short spell. When I came to, the plane was about fifty feet from the ground."

"You're a survivor," Jamal said. "And the survivor in you told you to wake up."

"Maybe so." Mr. Hawkins smiled at his son. "At the last second, I managed to control the crash somewhat and keep the plane from total devastation."

"Then what?" Joe asked eagerly.

"After the crash," Mr. Hawkins continued, "I looked back to see how Fairbanks was. But he was gone. Then I realized he had probably bailed out when I was unconscious. No fun riding a plane when the pilot is sleeping."

66

"What did you do next?" Jamal asked.

"Well, the front explosion took my radio out, so I couldn't call for help," Mr. Hawkins said. "And I was afraid the rear explosion had taken out my ELT, which would make it hard for the air patrol to find me. My right arm and leg were both injured, so I decided to stay where I was. I shot off a flare, bundled a tarp around me for warmth, and waited."

"So you just waited there for twenty-four hours?" Joe asked, admiring the man's fortitude.

"The pain got so bad that I drifted in and out of consciousness," Mr. Hawkins said. "And the cold was starting to give me hypothermia. Then a few hours ago, an air force Talon found me. Good thing, too. I don't know if I could have made it much longer."

"Do you think something just went wrong with your plane?" Joe asked. "Or was it sabotaged?"

"Frankly, I think it was sabotaged," Mr. Hawkins answered. "I think there were two time-activated bombs placed on the plane. They must have been carefully hidden, though, because I didn't catch them in any of my preflight checks."

"Sounds like the same clever weasel who fixed my Cessna," Jamal put in.

"If the bombs were time-activated," Joe said thoughtfully, "that means they could have been placed on the plane either in Ottawa or in Bayport."

67

"You're awfully interested in this, aren't you?" Mr. Hawkins commented.

Jamal then explained everything to his father—about the Hardys being detectives, about finding the journal, about the close call in the Cessna.

"Well, I see my son has made some interesting friends," Mr. Hawkins finally said.

"Did Ian Fairbanks say anything about who might want to kill him?" Joe asked.

"No, he didn't," Mr. Hawkins replied.

"Did you ask Fairbanks if he knew Dexter Cross?" Joe asked.

"I did," Mr. Hawkins said. "Fairbanks said he'd never heard of him. But then, Fairbanks couldn't know everyone who receives payments from each branch of his corporation. From what you've told me about Cross though, it sounds like he's up to something."

"What about Ken McCafferty?" Joe inquired. "If Cross is involved with something illegal, do you think McCafferty could be in on it?"

"I never thought so," Mr. Hawkins said. "But the fact is, there is a skeleton in Ken's closet."

"What's that?" Joe asked.

"Ken was a fighter pilot in the force," Mr. Hawkins explained. "Just like me. But he had some bad luck. His eyesight went from perfect to twenty-eighty. No big deal for most pilots, but the air force has very strict regulations, and they wouldn't let him fly anymore. Ken begged them to bend the rules for him, but they couldn't."

68

"Boy, that must have been a big blow to him," Joe said sympathetically.

"So he quit the force?" Jamal asked.

"They offered him a ground job at the base of his choice," Mr. Hawkins said. "But Ken was mad. He's a flyer and he wanted to fly. Late one night he sneaked an F-16 out of the hangar and went out on a joy ride. When the brass found out about it, he was dishonorably discharged. They took away his medals, and he gets no pension."

"How did he come to you?" Joe asked.

"Just came in looking for a job," Mr. Hawkins said. "He told me the full story about his discharge and how that kept him from getting a job with a commercial airline. He seemed like a decent guy who just used some bad judgment one night. So I hired him. And I've liked Ken ever since."

"I don't know whether to feel bad for him or watch my back around him," Jamal said thoughtfully.

"Maybe both," Joe said.

"Now that you've found me," Mr. Hawkins asked Joe, "do you plan to keep working on the case?"

"You better believe it," Joe responded. "Ian Fairbanks could die in the mountains. And attempts have been made on all of our lives. My brother and I want this guy. Matter of fact, we want him bad."

"Please be careful," Mr. Hawkins advised. "I'm sure your dad would tell you the same thing."

"I know," Joe said with a smile. He stood and

stretched. "Well, I'd better turn in. I'm flying back to D.C. first thing tomorrow morning. I want to pay another visit to the airport where we parked the Cessna. Maybe I can find a clue."

"If I don't see you tomorrow," Jamal told Joe, "I'll catch you in a few days. And thanks for being there, man. I mean it."

Joe gave Jamal and Mr. Hawkins a thumbs-up sign, then left the room.

Around midnight, three hundred miles south of Plattsburgh, Frank arrived at the Bayport train station and took a taxi to the Bayport Airport. The taxi let him off at the end of a line of yellow cabs parked in front of the main airport building.

Frank walked over to a group of cab drivers who were clustered together near their cars. "Anyone here named Sammy?" Frank asked.

"I'm Sammy," said a short man wearing a hunting cap with the ear flaps down.

Frank introduced himself. "Betty thought you could help me with some information," he explained. "She said you used to work for Tamara Fairbanks."

Sammy signaled Frank, and together they moved away from the cluster of drivers. "So what is it you want to know?" Sammy asked.

"I hear Tamara Fairbanks fired you as chauffeur because she said she was expecting some trouble and needed a bodyguard," Frank said. "Do you know what sort of trouble she was referring to?"

"You see, when I went to work for Ms. Fairbanks," Sammy explained, "she made me sign a form promising I wouldn't talk about anything I overheard. And since I don't want to be prosecuted, I can't actually say anything about her. But if you want to know about the trouble, you might try Mr. Abernathy. You can find him most mornings on the golf course of the Bayport Country Club. Even in the winter."

"The Bayport Country Club," Frank repeated. "Thanks a mil, Sammy."

"Hey, do me a favor," Sammy said. "Say hi to Betty for me."

"You got it," Frank promised.

Frank hurried across the airport grounds to the Hawkins Air Service hangar, where Jamal's car was parked. Since the van was in the shop, Jamal had given Frank the keys to his car. Frank noticed another car parked near Jamal's and wondered if someone was in the hangar. He tried the side door to the hangar and found it open.

By the light of a fluorescent lamp on Betty's desk, Frank could see the shapes of lockers and planes across the hangar. He seemed to be alone.

When Frank wandered back to Mr. Hawkins's office, he was surprised to find Ken McCafferty sitting there, his arms and head resting on the desk. The pilot's eyes were open, but he seemed dazed.

"Mr. McCafferty," Frank said quietly. The pilot slowly looked up. "What are you doing here?"

71

Frank asked. "I thought you weren't scheduled to bring Cross back until tomorrow."

McCafferty stared at Frank as though seeing a ghost. Then McCafferty shook his head, as if to clear out the cobwebs. "Cross finished his business early," McCafferty said, "so I brought him back this afternoon. I'm surprised to see *you* here."

"Jamal is lending me his car, and I came by to pick it up," Frank explained. "You've heard about Mr. Hawkins, I guess."

"Yeah, Betty told me," McCafferty said, running a hand through his cropped brown hair. "I jumped for joy when I heard the boss was okay."

"Yeah, it's great news," Frank said.

"Where are your partners in crime?" McCafferty asked. "Joe and Jamal."

"They're with Mr. Hawkins in Plattsburgh," Frank answered. "I'm not sure when they're coming back."

"Plattsburgh, huh?" McCafferty muttered.

Keeping in mind that McCafferty was now a suspect, Frank decided not to tell the pilot anything more about the day's adventures.

"Pretty impressive the way the air force found that plane in the snow," Frank said, keeping the conversation casual.

"Yeah, the good ol' air force," McCafferty said, getting up from the desk. "Too good for me I guess."

"What do you mean?" Frank asked.

"Oh, let's just say the force and I didn't see eye

72

to eye," McCafferty said, stretching his arms. "But, hey, I've got a pretty good job with Mr. Hawkins. Excuse me, kid. I'm going to get some coffee before I fall asleep."

McCafferty gave a casual salute, then left the room. Frank sat there a moment, listening to the winter wind howl outside. He thought McCafferty sounded a little bitter as he talked about the air force. What could that be about, Frank wondered.

Suddenly the office was plunged into darkness as the lights went out! Before Frank could move, he heard a scuffle in the hangar.

"Hey! Hey! What are you doing!" he heard McCafferty shout. Then Frank heard McCafferty scream as if he was in great pain.

Frank felt his way out of the office only to find that the rest of the hangar also pitch-black. "Mr. McCafferty?" Frank called as he groped his way through the darkness. "Ken, are you okay?"

Then, out of nowhere, Frank felt a sharp karate chop to the back of his neck!

8 The Lost Ticket

Frank fell to his knees, dazed. He thought he heard footsteps echoing through the hangar and fading away. Then he blacked out.

A few moments later Frank was aware of the fluorescent light over Betty's desk and the dim shapes of the airplane hangar. The wind rattled against the steel ceiling, and Frank slowly realized Ken McCafferty was standing over him.

"Welcome back, kid," McCafferty said. "Somebody flipped the circuit breaker. That's why it went dark. Then someone grabbed me from behind. I wrestled with him, and I guess he got me with a knife. He went for you next, but I chased after him and he took off running. Whoever it was."

Frank noticed there was a nasty gash on McCafferty's cheek. "We'd better take care of that cut," Frank said, sitting up slowly.

McCafferty touched the blood on his cheek. "You stay put. I'll get the first-aid kit," he said, heading for a locker.

Frank was confused. Ten minutes ago McCafferty was looking like a prime suspect, but now he seemed more like another victim. Who was the intruder with the knife? Frank's thoughts were swimming inside his pounding head. He realized he desperately needed a good night's sleep.

Early the next morning, Joe flew a commercial flight back to Washington, D.C., then caught a cab to the auxiliary airport, where the Cessna had been parked the day before. Joe wandered up and down the tarmac, hoping to find a clue about who had tampered with the Cessna.

Then Joe saw a maintenance vehicle rolling slowly along the tarmac. A gray-haired man in a jumpsuit was behind the wheel.

"Excuse me, sir," Joe called, running up to the vehicle. "Were you on duty yesterday afternoon?"

The maintenance man pulled a lever and stopped the truck. "Yes, I was," the man replied.

"Do you remember a plane parked in this area that was covered with a tarp?" Joe asked.

"Yes, I do," the man said. "I've got a good memory. It was a gray tarp, and the plane was sitting right over there." He pointed across the tarmac.

"Did you see someone working on the plane?" Joe asked.

"Well, I might have," the man answered. "Around noon, I saw a man slip under the tarp. Then about ten minutes later I noticed him slip back out."

"What did he look like?" Joe asked, his heart speeding up with excitement.

"My memory may be good, but my eyesight is pretty bad," the man admitted. "Besides, I only saw him from a distance."

"Do you remember anything about him," Joe urged. "What was he wearing? A trenchcoat, maybe?"

"I'm sorry"—the man shrugged—"I couldn't tell you. I just don't make out details too well."

"Thanks, anyway," Joe said with disappointment.

"Oh, wait," the maintenance man said suddenly. "I almost forgot. Soon after the man left, I found an airplane ticket lying right by the tarp. It must have fallen out of his pocket."

"What did you do with it?" Joe asked eagerly.

"I took it to the lost and found, of course," the man said. "What else would I do with it?"

After thanking the man, Joe ran to the lost and found booth and claimed the only lost ticket booklet they had. Joe also learned that no one else had picked up a lost ticket recently.

Inside the ticket booklet Joe found a round-trip

ticket from Bayport to Los Angeles for tomorrow morning, Saturday. The ticket was in the name of Pat Buchman.

This could be a significant break in the case, Joe thought. *And we sure do need a break.* He figured Pat Buchman was an assumed name, and the owner of this ticket was probably the person who had sabotaged the Cessna. And the person who sabotaged the Cessna was probably the same person who had sabotaged the plane with Ian Fairbanks on it. Would this person be on the flight to L.A. tomorrow?

Joe hurried to a pay phone and called the airline that issued the ticket. "Hello, my name is Pat Buchman," Joe lied. "I bought a ticket for tomorrow's flight 231, Bayport to Los Angeles, but I've lost the ticket. Can I still take the flight?"

"Not without your ticket," the airline rep said. Joe's heart sank. "However," the rep continued, "my computer readout shows that you have purchased a second ticket for that very same flight."

"Oh, good," Joe said, covering quickly. "My secretary must have done that after I told her that I had lost the ticket. And what is my seat assignment, please?"

"That's 21-A, sir," the airline rep replied.

After he hung up, Joe wrote "21-A" on the ticket booklet. Then he noticed something else. There was something already scribbled on the back: "Meet X at Gory Gulch Sat. 5PM."

This must mean Passenger 21-A was meeting someone at that specific site tomorrow afternoon. Joe immediately called Frank in Bayport to relay the news, but no one was home except Aunt Gertrude.

"Joe Hardy, where are you?" Aunt Gertrude demanded. Aunt Gertrude lived with the Hardy family. Sometimes Joe thought her favorite hobby was worrying about the Hardy brothers, especially when Mr. and Mrs. Hardy were out of town, as they were now.

"I'm in Washington D.C.," Joe said. "But I'm coming back on the next flight. I should be home in time for dinner."

"I should hope so," Aunt Gertrude said. "I'm planning to make your favorite mashed potatoes."

As soon as Joe got off the phone, he suddenly remembered—he and Frank still had not gotten Aunt Gertrude a Christmas present!

After a night of sleep, Frank felt refreshed and ready for action. His first stop was the Bayport Country Club. As he strolled onto the ninth green, he saw a distinguished-looking man with silvery hair drive up in a golf cart. Though the snow was melting, the golf course was still more white than green.

"Excuse me," Frank said, approaching the cart. "Are you Mr. Abernathy?"

"That's right," Mr. Abernathy replied as he stepped out of the golf cart.

"I'm Frank Hardy, and I was told you could tell me something about Tamara Fairbanks."

"You want some dirt on her, I bet," Abernathy said, pulling a club from his golf bag.

"I just want the truth."

"Well," Abernathy said, looking straight at Frank, "it depends on whose side you're on. . . ."

Frank wasn't sure what to make of this, but he knew an opening when he saw one. "I'm not on anybody's side," he said, hedging. "I'm just trying to find out who's behind an attempt on her father's life."

"Oh, yes," Abernathy said, walking to the tee-off point. "I read about his disappearance in the paper this morning."

Frank followed Abernathy. "What can you tell me about Tamara Fairbanks?"

Abernathy pulled a red golf ball from his pocket and set it on a tee. He swung a few practice strokes. "The reason I play golf every morning," Abernathy explained, "is because I have nothing better to do. I used to be the president of a major corporation. But two years ago Tamara Fairbanks masterminded a hostile takeover of my company. Do you know what that means?"

"She managed to buy up over fifty percent of the company's stock," Frank answered, "giving herself power to do whatever she wanted with the company. Including getting rid of the president. So now you play golf every morning."

"Very good." Abernathy smirked, "My contacts

in the business world have informed me that Ms. Fairbanks is planning a takeover of an even bigger company—the Fairbanks Corporation.''

Frank paused a moment. ''You mean,'' Frank said with disbelief, ''she's planning a takeover of her father's own company? A company that she herself works for?''

''That's what I hear,'' Abernathy confirmed. ''Very few people know about this, but I understand she's been working on it behind her father's back for the past year or so.''

''Isn't her father too sharp to let this happen?'' Frank asked.

''If there's one person in this world more ruthless than Tamara Fairbanks,'' Abernathy proclaimed, ''it's her father, Ian. In fact, I hear he's hired a couple of spies to keep an eye on Tamara. But the Fairbanks Corporation is in serious debt these days, and unless Fairbanks senior can come up with some pretty hefty capital, he may not be able to stop his daughter's takeover bid.''

''He won't be able to stop it if he's dead either,'' Frank said. ''Which brings me to my last question. Do you think Tamara Fairbanks tried to kill her father so she could win this takeover game?''

''I couldn't say,'' Abernathy shook his head. ''But I sure wouldn't put it past her.''

Frank spent the rest of the day following other leads, and when he got home around six, Joe was already there. Though Mr. and Mrs. Hardy were out of town for the weekend, Joe had spoken briefly with his father on the phone about the current case.

After a quick dinner with Aunt Gertrude, the Hardys went upstairs to review all their information. "Someone has tried to kill me, you, Jamal, and Mr. Hawkins, and they may have already killed Ian Fairbanks," Joe said, clutching a football. "Come on, Frank, who could it be?"

"This afternoon," Frank related, "I tried to check on what Fairbanks was doing in Ottawa, and whom Tamara may be conspiring with on the takeover, and which Fairbanks subsidiary was issuing checks to Cross. But nobody in the corporate world was talking."

"Dad said the police and the FBI can research that stuff better than us," Joe said, tossing Frank the football. "So let's try to figure out who could have sabotaged our plane and the plane Ian Fairbanks was on. Who could have known about the flights?"

"The most likely people are the employees of Hawkins Air Service," Frank pointed out. "There's Betty, Ken, several other pilots, and a mechanic."

"And I talked to them all this afternoon when I got back from D.C.," Joe said. "They all seemed okay. McCafferty seemed to be the most likely suspect of the bunch. Except the same person who attacked you last night in the hangar also attacked him."

"Boys?" Aunt Gertrude called from her bedroom

81

down the hall. "Would you look at the front yard? There's a strange man out there."

Immediately Joe flipped off the light switch so he and his brother wouldn't be visible through the window. Frank moved to the window, pulled back the curtain, and looked down at the front yard below.

A black limousine was parked out by the curb. There was a man leaning against the limo, and though it was dark, Frank knew exactly who it was.

"Frankenstein," Joe whispered behind Frank. Then Joe saw the chauffeur reach inside his suit jacket and pull something out.

That something was a pistol!

9 Merry Christmas, from Frank to Joe

Despite the darkness, Joe could swear he saw the chauffeur's lips form into a smile as he withdrew his pistol.

"Joe, get back," Frank urged as he moved away from the window. "Bullets travel awfully fast."

"Supersonic," Joe said, joining Frank up against their bedroom wall.

Joe was dying to see what the chauffeur was doing, but he didn't dare move into the line of fire. Soon he heard the sound of a car engine starting out by the curb. He got to the window in time to see the limousine driving off into the night.

"Well, that was fun," Joe said, picking up the football again. "What do you make of it?"

"He's trying to scare us away from Tamara Fairbanks," Frank said thoughtfully. "Obviously the

83

lady plays rough, but we still don't have anything that connects her to her father's disappearance. In fact, we don't have anything that connects anybody to Ian Fairbanks's disappearance. That's our problem."

"You know what our best lead is?" Joe said, pacing the room with the football under his arm. "That airplane ticket. We're pretty sure the person who sabotaged the Cessna and probably Fairbanks's trip from Ottawa is going to be passenger 21-A on that flight to Los Angeles tomorrow."

"All right," Frank said, rubbing his forehead. "Why don't we go to the gate tomorrow morning? If we see one of our suspects there, we'll notify the authorities to pick up the trail in L.A. If we don't see anyone we know, I'll take the flight myself and find out exactly who's in seat 21-A."

"How come you get to go?" Joe protested.

"Because I'm older," Frank said, snatching the football from Joe.

At nine o'clock the next morning, Frank and Joe entered the main terminal building of the Bayport Airport. The place was a whirling kaleidoscope of people, luggage, and television monitors lit up with flight information.

"It's crazy in here," Joe said, dodging bodies. "It must be the Christmas blitz."

"We'd better check on my ticket," Frank said.

The Hardys took their place at the end of a long

line at a ticket counter. Joe pulled the morning edition of the *Bayport Gazette* from his shoulder bag. The headline read: "Millionaire Missing Two Days."

"It says," Joe said, skimming the paper, "the Civil Air Patrol and the air force are still searching for Fairbanks in the Adirondacks. It also says the police and FBI have no proof that someone was attempting to assassinate Fairbanks."

Peering over Joe's shoulder, Frank saw the same photograph of Ian Fairbanks he had seen at the Fairbanks store. "I still say he looks like he's watching us," Frank observed. "Look at those eyes."

As the Hardys neared the front of the line, Frank glanced around the busy terminal. "Joe, look," Frank said, nudging his brother.

Joe followed Frank's gaze to the shops and fast food counters across the terminal. He spotted Tamara Fairbanks at a newsstand reading a paper. Her chauffeur stood nearby, holding a small suitcase.

"Is she coming or going?" Joe wondered aloud.

"Maybe she's going to L.A.," Frank said, "and she's Pat Buchman. If she's going to work on the takeover plot, she might want to use an alias."

"Maybe," Joe agreed. "Her chauffeur could have had her ticket and dropped it after tampering with our Cessna in D.C."

"We're next in line," Frank said, handing Joe his

airplane ticket. "You confirm the flight. I'll go after Tamara. She's paying for her paper, and I don't want to lose track of her."

Frank began moving through the sea of bodies toward the newsstand. Waiting for her change, Tamara suddenly glanced in Frank's direction. Oh, no, Frank thought, she saw me.

Tamara dropped the newspaper and walked away from the newsstand. Frank saw she was making a beeline for the exit, with the chauffeur right behind her. Maybe she doesn't want me to know she's going to L.A., Frank thought, so she's trying to lose me. Luckily, Frankenstein is about a head taller than most people, so the big goon is easy to tail.

"Wait," Frank yelled, trotting after Tamara. "I have to talk with you!"

The chauffeur wheeled around and headed for Frank. Frank tried to circle around him, but the big man suddenly swung the suitcase, catching Frank hard in the stomach. Frank reeled back a step, his shoulder bag flying off his shoulder.

"Stay away from her," the chauffeur growled, blocking Frank's path.

"Afraid I can't do that," Frank returned.

Frank made a fake to his right. The chauffeur went for it, and Frank dodged left, chasing after Tamara, who was now approaching the exit doors. Then Frank realized he had left his shoulder bag behind.

"Tamara," Frank called. "Wait, please. It's important. It's about your father!"

Frank ran back to get his bag, but by the time he retrieved it, the chauffeur had rejoined Tamara, and they were just stepping through the automatic glass doors. Frank dashed after them and managed to catch up with them at the limousine.

"Hey!" Frank called, attempting to stop Tamara. "Aren't you going to miss your flight?"

Tamara turned to Frank. "Not that it's any of your business," Tamara snapped, "but I have just landed."

"Any chance I could see your ticket?" Frank asked.

The chauffeur opened the backseat door of the limo. Ignoring Frank, Tamara started to get inside.

"If you show it to me," Frank called, "I won't spread the word that you're planning a hostile takeover of a company that bears your family name."

Tamara's eyes shot icicles at Frank. A moment passed. "Get in the car," Tamara said firmly.

Frank had to think twice about this. If he got in the limo, there was a chance he would never get out of it alive. On the other hand, this could be his only chance to find out if Tamara Fairbanks was passenger 21-A. Deciding to risk it, Frank climbed into the backseat. Tamara got in after him, and the chauffeur took his place behind the wheel.

"How much do you want?" Tamara demanded, as the chauffeur navigated through the airport traffic.

"What are you talking about?" Frank said, sinking into the soft leather of the roomy backseat.

"How much money do you want to keep all of this quiet?" Tamara asked.

"All of what?" Frank asked, wanting her to be more specific.

"How much is my father paying you?" Tamara said. "I'll double it."

"How much is your father . . . ?" Frank said, puzzled. "What do you mean?"

"Look," Tamara stated, "I know you and your pal are spies my father has hired to keep an eye on me. I've seen two men following me for the past six months, but I didn't get a close look at you and your partner until the other evening."

"When we came to your office and then followed you?" Frank asked.

"That's right," Tamara responded. "How fitting that my father would hire a couple of teenagers. Anything to cut down on the tremendous debt he has created."

"Your father suspects you of trying to take over his corporation," Frank said, trying to make sense of things. "So he put spies on you. And that's why you hired a more, uh, threatening chauffeur. So he could scare the spies away."

"Exactly," Tamara confirmed. "But apparently he may have to do something more than just scare you this time."

Frank caught the chauffeur watching him in the rearview mirror. Frank also noticed the limo was now on the outskirts of the airport.

"A father spying on his daughter," Frank said.

88

"A daughter who tries to take over her father's company. Doesn't sound like one big happy family, does it?"

"It's not," Tamara said, turning to stare out the window.

"I've heard Ian Fairbanks isn't a very nice man," Frank dared to say. "I can see how the resentment would build up year after year until one day you decide you want the old man out of the picture."

Frank's bold attempt to get Tamara to talk seemed to work. When she turned back to Frank, tears were moistening her mascara. "When I was your age," Tamara said, her voice tinged with bitterness, "my father never had ten minutes for me. He was always traveling the world, cutting deals, building the Fairbanks empire. When I came into the business he still barely gave me the time of day. Because I'm a woman, he never believed I could be a truly effective business mogul."

"So the takeover," Frank realized, "would be a way to get your father's attention and respect."

"In a way I'm sure you could never understand," Tamara said, "I'm only doing it because I love him."

"So you didn't arrange for his plane to go down in the mountains of upstate New York?" Frank asked.

"If my father is dead," Tamara said, wiping a tear from her cheek, "he'll never appreciate how brilliantly I've masterminded his downfall."

"Believe it or not, Ms. Fairbanks," Frank said

sympathetically, "I think I understand. And for the record, I'm not one of the spies your father has hired. I'm one of the people trying to find out what happened to him. By the way, do you know anyone by the name of Dexter Cross?"

"No," Tamara said, taking a shaky breath. "Sven, I believe this boy is harmless. Drop him where we found him, please."

A few minutes later, Frank rushed back inside the terminal and found Joe waiting anxiously with the ticket. "What did you find out?" Joe asked.

"Tamara Fairbanks isn't behind the sabotage," Frank said as the Hardys began moving through the crowd.

"Why do you say that?"

After hearing Frank's explanation, Joe said, "Your flight is confirmed. It leaves in twenty minutes. I'll go to the gate with you in case there's any trouble ahead."

Soon the Hardys came to a long line of travelers waiting to pass through the metal detectors. Finally they came to the front of the line. When a security guard gave the signal, Frank set his shoulder bag on the conveyor belt and watched it slide toward the X-ray machine. As Frank stepped through the metal detector, he passed another security guard carefully studying the X-ray monitor.

Next, Joe stepped through the metal detector. "Guess who's behind us?" he whispered to Frank.

Frank glanced back. At the end of the line he saw a man in an old overcoat and wrinkled khakis. It took Frank a second to realize the man was Dexter Cross, without his glasses. Cross didn't look the least bit like a financial consultant now.

"Would you care to explain this?" a security guard suddenly asked Frank. Frank noticed the guard was holding open his shoulder bag. To Frank's amazement, inside the bag he saw a small box tied with a bright red ribbon.

"What's that?" Joe asked Frank.

"I have no idea," Frank said, lifting the mysterious box from the bag.

On top of the box was a card that read: "Merry Christmas, from Frank to Joe." Frank quickly ripped off the ribbon and opened the box.

Inside was a Beretta pistol!

10 The Fighting Falcons

"Sir, you are under arrest," the guard announced, pulling out a pair of handcuffs and grabbing Frank's wrist.

"Joe," Frank said as the guard opened the cuffs, "take my ticket and don't miss the flight."

"Are you with him?" the guard asked Joe.

"Uh . . . yes, sir," Joe said hesitantly.

"Then you're not going anywhere either," the guard said.

Frank and Joe were both handcuffed. Soon two other guards appeared and marched the Hardys down a hallway and into a security room. The Hardys were ordered to sit and wait. Frank eyed his watch every few seconds, wondering if the plane would take off without him. After ten minutes had gone by, a dour-looking man in a dark suit finally entered the room.

"Boys," the man announced, sitting on the edge of the desk, "I am an official of the Federal Aviation Administration. And I'm here to tell you it's a violation of federal law to carry or attempt to carry firearms onto a commercial airliner."

"Sir, I didn't know the gun was there," Frank insisted. "I was set up."

"Call Con Riley of the Bayport Police," Joe added. "He'll explain to you that we're detectives and we're telling the truth about this."

"What sort of detectives are you?" the FAA man asked with an arched eyebrow.

"Call Officer Riley!" Joe burst out. "Please! One of us has to catch a flight in five minutes!"

The man picked up a phone, keeping his eyes on the Hardys, and soon he was having a lengthy discussion with Officer Con Riley. Finally he hung up the phone and signaled a guard to unhandcuff the Hardys.

"Officer Riley convinced me you boys are on the level," the FAA official said as the guard began unlocking Frank's cuffs. "Therefore, I'm letting you go with no charges. However, I'll be keeping the gun for fingerprinting."

"If you find any prints," Frank said, "please pass on the information to the Bayport Police. They're also working on this case."

"That's standard procedure," the FAA man said as a guard unlocked Joe's cuffs.

"Maybe you can still make the flight," Joe said to Frank.

The FAA official picked up the phone again and inquired about the flight. Hanging up, he said, "Sorry, boys, but your plane just took off."

"There goes passenger 21-A," Joe complained.

"Wait," Frank said. "Remember what was written on the ticket: 'Meet X at Gory Gulch Saturday five P.M.' Gory Gulch is bound to be somewhere near L.A. If we can get there in time, we might still find our man."

Joe scowled. "I doubt there's another plane leaving soon for L.A.," he said. "Besides, what is Gory Gulch? It could be a town, a canyon, anything."

"I know," Frank said, pulling a slip of paper from his wallet. "I'll call Jamal at the Plattsburgh base. Maybe he can find Gory Gulch on one of the military maps there. Mind if I use the phone?" he asked the FAA man.

"Be my guest," he said.

Frank managed to reach Jamal at the Plattsburgh base and explained the situation to him. Jamal said he'd see what he could do, and twenty minutes later he called back.

"I had to scour this map," Jamal told Frank, "but I finally found Gory Gulch. It's an old mining town about seventy miles northeast of L.A."

"Great," Frank said, taking notes.

"It gets better," Jamal said. "I called General Radman at Andrews. I won't hold you up with the details, but transportation west has been arranged for you. Haul yourselves to McGuire Air Force Base. It's about an hour away, just south of Trenton, New Jersey. You'll be met at the gate. You should get to California in plenty of time to track your prey."

"Excellent," Frank said, still writing.

"And one more thing," Jamal added. "Man-oh-man, are you guys lucky!"

An hour and a half later, the Hardys drove Jamal's car through the front gate of McGuire Air Force Base. They were met by an air force sergeant.

"Drive straight ahead," the sergeant instructed as he got into the car. "We have two F-16s here scheduled to fly today to a base near Los Angeles. These are two-seater training planes so, at the request of General Radman, we are going to let you boys hitch a ride."

"F-16s!" Joe cried in excitement. "Those are the Fighting Falcons we saw yesterday."

"Jamal told us we were lucky," Frank said, "and he was right."

Soon, Frank and Joe, wearing helmets and green flight suits, were walking across the tarmac toward two dark-gray F-16 fighter jets. Two young pilots, also in flight gear, were waiting for them, and Joe noticed one of them was female.

"I'm She-wolf," the female pilot said, referring to her flyer nickname. "And this is Tiger. Hope you're ready for an exciting ride."

Frank climbed into one cockpit, and Joe climbed

into the other. Tiger helped Frank strap in—two straps crisscrossing the chest and another strap across the waist—and She-wolf helped Joe. Then the pilots helped each Hardy get his oxygen mask in place.

"The mask will keep you breathing okay," She-wolf told Joe. "If you get dizzy, let me know."

She-wolf climbed into the seat in front of Joe, and Tiger sat in front of Frank. After the preflight checks, clear plastic "canopies" lowered over the tiny cockpits.

Next, the Hardys listened to the radio communication through their headsets. "Andrews tower," Tiger radioed, "this is zulu-eight-one-four requesting clearance for takeoff."

"You are clear for takeoff, zulu-eight-one-four," a voice replied.

Frank heard a jet engine burning its intense power behind him, then felt the F-16 charging down the runway—faster, faster, faster—and thrust upward into the open air. A force pushed him deep into his seat. At once, the world around Frank was a panorama of sky, clouds, grass, trees, all whizzing by at an amazing speed.

Frank took a deep breath in his mask. "How fast will we be flying?" Frank spoke into a mike in the mask.

"We can't fly supersonic over populated areas," Tiger said, "but we'll go fast enough."

"Hey, brother," Frank heard in his headset. "It's Joe. How's it going in there?"

Frank looked out his canopy and saw the other F-16 soaring right beside him. "It's going just fine, bro," Frank said into his mike as he waved.

"You'll be experiencing a little G-force," Tiger told Frank. "Let me introduce you to it."

"Sure," Frank said, knowing that G-force meant the weight of gravity pushing against a body.

"You feel the G-force," Tiger explained, "with a sudden acceleration like on the takeoff or when we bank or turn at high speed. Like this."

Suddenly the plane banked to the right, and Frank felt a pressure against his face and chest. It felt as if Joe was pushing on him in a wrestling match.

"That's two Gs," Tiger said. "Let's try three."

As Tiger banked the plane more sharply, it felt as if both Joe *and* Chet were pushing on Frank with all their might. Then the plane straightened, and at once the pressure eased away.

"Wouldn't want any more than three," Frank said.

"I've pulled nine Gs before," Tiger bragged. "It's pretty rough. Don't worry, you shouldn't feel any more than three on this trip."

Within twenty minutes, they were soaring over the skyscrapers of Pittsburgh. "How long do you have to train to fly these planes?" Frank asked.

"Two years," Tiger replied. "And you have to be pretty good just to get into the F-16 program."

Over the next forty minutes, Frank watched a

97

string of cities and towns give way to the rolling farms and wheat fields of the midwestern plains.

"Awesome way to see the country!" Frank said.

"Yep," Tiger agreed, "the only way to travel."

In another twenty minutes, the Falcons landed at Whiteman Air Force Base in Kansas City for a brief refueling, and then they zoomed off into the sky again. Forty minutes later Joe was looking down at the snowcapped peaks of the Rocky Mountains.

"Have you flown in a battle situation?" Joe asked She-wolf.

"Not yet," She-wolf answered. "But if the time comes to defend my country, I am certainly ready."

"I'll bet you are," Joe said with admiration.

Thirty minutes later Joe gazed down at the monumental splendor of the Grand Canyon. "Can I stop for a picture?" Joe joked.

"Sorry, no time," She-wolf replied with a laugh.

Soon Joe saw the Mojave Desert sprawled out below, vast and sand-colored, looking like the surface of an alien planet.

"Tiger," She-wolf radioed, "now that we're over the desert, how 'bout we take these boys supersonic?"

"Roger, She-wolf," Tiger radioed back.

Suddenly the jet engine burned louder, and Joe felt a slight increase in G-force pressure. Then the desert flew by in an awesome rush of motion. For a moment there was quiet, and Joe noticed a bluish haze surrounding the outside of the plane.

"Did we just break the sound barrier?" he asked.

"Congratulations," She-wolf said. "You're now flying faster than the speed of sound. It's pretty smooth in an F-16, but in the old days the planes would shake like mad when they went supersonic. Those pilots must have been crazy back then."

Ten minutes later the two F-16s came roaring down the runway of an air force facility in Palmdale, California. As the engine died down to silence, Joe's body buzzed all over from the amazing journey.

"She-wolf," Joe said, a big grin on his face. "That might have been the best three hours of my life. Thanks for the ride."

"Thank your Uncle Sam," She-wolf replied.

After the Hardys got out of their flight suits, they were met by a Sergeant Lewin, a young airman who had been instructed by General Radman to see to the Hardys' needs. He had agreed to give the Hardys dirt bikes and a map so they could arrive at Gory Gulch on time.

"What time is your appointment?" Sergeant Lewin asked.

"Five o'clock," Frank said, adjusting his watch. "But it's just two o'clock Pacific time so we're ahead of schedule."

"Let's take a walk," Sergeant Lewin suggested. "You need to stretch your legs after that flight."

The Hardys had left their coats at McGuire Air Force Base and they now rolled up their sleeves, enjoying the warm California sunshine. Sergeant Lewin brought them to a guard station manned by

99

four air force security policemen in camouflage fatigues. Joe took one look at the security cops and knew they meant business.

After Sergeant Lewin spoke with a police officer, he escorted the Hardys through the gate. If Andrews Air Force Base resembled a suburban neighborhood, Frank observed, the Palmdale base resembled an industrial complex. All around were large rectangular buildings that looked like warehouses. Frank noticed none of the buildings had windows.

"What goes on at this base?" Joe inquired.

"Palmdale is a unique air force facility," Sergeant Lewin explained. "This is where civilian contractors do research and build airplanes for the air force."

"I guess that's why the security is so tight," Frank said. Air force police officers were posted in front of every one of the buildings.

"Much of the work done here is highly classified," Sergeant Lewin said as they continued walking. "I was only able to get you past that guard station because General Radman okayed it."

"I heard a rumor that the air force has a hypersonic plane they're test-flying in Nevada," Joe said. "Do you know if there's any truth to that?"

Sergeant Lewin hesitated. "All I can say is, the air force is exploring the possibility of hypersonic flight."

The Hardys were now in front of a gigantic building the size of a city block. Joe noticed a large supply truck parked at a loading dock around the side of the building. Men were unloading what looked like long metal cylinders from the truck.

"What's this huge building for?" Frank asked.

"It's an assembly building," Sergeant Lewin answered. "Airplanes are put together piece by piece inside. There are probably eight hundred people working behind those doors at the moment."

"Do you know what type of plane is being built in there now?" Frank asked, fishing for details.

"Sorry," Sergeant Lewin said. "That's classified information."

Just then Frank realized Joe was gone. He looked around quickly, spotting his brother headed for the building's loading dock. He figured Joe wanted to see what exactly was being unloaded from the truck. He also figured it was a bad idea.

The next moment, Sergeant Lewin also saw Joe.

"Stop!" Sergeant Lewin screamed. Then he began running toward Joe, frantically waving his arms.

"Stop, stop, stop!"

11 A Drink at the Oasis

Joe whipped around when he heard Sergeant Lewin shouting at him. He was shocked to see four air force policemen descending on him, each with a hand on his holster. "I surrender," Joe said, his hands up.

"What are you doing?" Sergeant Lewin demanded when he reached Joe.

"I just wanted to see what those things were," Joe said, gesturing at the long cylinders still being unloaded from the nearby truck.

"I told you," Sergeant Lewin scolded, "the work that goes on here is highly classified!"

"And my brother," Frank said, joining the group, "is *highly* curious."

"It's all right," Sergeant Lewin told the police officers. "The situation is under control." Sergeant

Lewin pulled a handkerchief from his pocket and mopped his brow. "Boys, I think we'd better end this tour now. I don't want you to be late for your appointment."

Twenty minutes later Frank and Joe were on a pair of dirt bikes roaring side by side down a desert highway. They wore sunglasses and windbreakers that Sergeant Lewin had generously loaned them.

The Mojave Desert, which the boys had just viewed from the sky, now lay all around them. The gently sloping landscape was a vast expanse of sand, rock, and gravel. Scattered along the desert floor were small shrubs and oddly twisting trees that Frank recognized as Joshua trees. Even though it was December, the sun glared across the desert with intense rays of heat.

"They take their security pretty seriously at that place," Joe yelled from his bike.

"You never know," Frank yelled back. "Those cylinders may be some top secret part that took twenty years to perfect. Don't forget, the air force sponsors the most cutting-edge research in aeronautic technology today."

Up close, the desert looked even more like a foreign planet than it had from the sky. The strange dunes and craters and caves of the Mojave reminded Joe of his recent visit to the surface of Mars exhibit at the Smithsonian.

"Wouldn't want to get lost out here," Joe called.

After an hour of cruising, the Hardys turned off the highway and roared down a series of narrow roads until they came to a bullet-riddled sign announcing Gory Gulch. They stopped and looked around. There was nothing to see but a cluster of rocky caverns.

"Where's Gory Gulch?" Joe asked.

"I think this is it," Frank replied. He pointed out several dilapidated shacks in the distance. They looked like something from the last century. Then Frank saw a café that looked only about thirty years old. He could just make out the word *Oasis* on a weathered sign hanging over the door.

The sun was beginning to dip in the western sky. "It's a quarter till five," Frank said, checking his watch. "No one's here yet."

"Believe it or not," Joe said, "I think that café is open. Why don't we wait there?"

Frank and Joe rode up to the café, parked their bikes around back, then went through a squeaky screen door into the Oasis. Inside the small café, there was a counter, several tables, and some aged photographs of airplanes on the wall.

"Howdy," a man behind the counter said. He was a grizzled man of about seventy, with weathered lines running across his face like those on a contour map. Joe noticed he wore a faded flight suit. "The name's Astro-Surfer. How can I help you?"

"Two colas, please," Frank said as he and Joe moved to a table by the window. An old set of venetian blinds were pulled down across the window to keep out the harsh desert sun.

"So this is a mining town," Joe remarked.

"That's right," Astro-Surfer said, bringing two cans of soda to the table. "There's a lot of these old ghost towns in the Mojave, but this is one of the least picturesque. Most of my customers stop by just because they're lost." Astro-Surfer grinned a smile of yellow teeth, then went back to the counter.

"Almost five," Frank said, checking his watch.

"And I think I see something," Joe said, peering through a slat of the venetian blinds.

A dark green Range Rover appeared on the horizon, a plume of desert dust in its wake. Joe watched it drive to the Gory Gulch sign and stop. A stocky, bald man wearing a sport shirt and sunglasses got out of the Rover and stood beside it. He was holding a satchel, Joe noticed.

"Doesn't look like anyone we know," Frank commented, also peering through the blinds.

"But, wait," Joe said, squinting to see better, "I think someone else is coming."

Through the blinds, the Hardys watched a dust cloud on the desert horizon grow larger until a red pickup truck emerged. Before long it also pulled up to the Gory Gulch sign.

A man stepped out of the truck. He wore a leather flight jacket and aviator sunglasses. "It's Ken McCafferty," Joe whispered.

"They're coming this way," Frank said, noticing the two men now heading straight for the Oasis.

"Astro-Surfer," Joe said as he and Frank moved away from the window, carrying their colas, "my

105

brother and I would like to surprise these guys. Is there a place we could hide in here?"

"There's a pantry through there." Astro-Surfer grinned, pointing to a door. "Help yourself. In the name of a good surprise, I won't say a word."

"Thanks," Frank said as the Hardys stepped through the pantry door. They found themselves in a room with flour, crackers, tin cans, and other dry goods. Ever so slightly, Joe cracked open the door, Frank right behind him.

Soon the Hardys heard the squeaky screen door of the Oasis open. "Howdy," the Hardys heard Astro-Surfer say. "What can I get you gents?"

"How about two colas?" Ken McCafferty asked.

"Coming up," Astro-Surfer replied.

Through the crack of the pantry door, Joe saw McCafferty and the stocky bald man sit at a table. Joe noticed a bandage on McCafferty's cheek. Without a word, the bald man put the satchel on the table and McCafferty took it. Then McCafferty put an envelope on the table and the bald man took that.

"You're a good man, Leach," McCafferty said.

"Shhhh," Leach whispered nervously.

"Sorry." McCafferty chuckled. "I mean Mr. X."

Astro-Surfer set two cans of soda on the table. "I'll be outside," Astro-Surfer said. "There's nothing to steal so I won't worry." With a wink, Astro-Surfer stepped out the door.

Right away the man called Leach leaned forward, and Joe opened the door a little wider to listen.

"There may not be anything to steal in this dump," Leach whispered, "but I've stolen some priceless information from the Palmdale facility. Well, you've got it all now, and I sure hope nothing goes wrong."

McCafferty took a sip of soda. "Listen," he said, setting down his soda can. "The reason I came two days late is I ran into some trouble. Your name is still clear, but these two kids may be onto me soon. I figure I should leave the country for good."

"When?" Leach asked.

"I'm taking off at oh-seven-thirty tomorrow," McCafferty said. "This guy sold me an old cargo plane, which he's leaving for me at Widow's Dry Lake. It's in an isolated part of Death Valley, so no one will see the plane take off from there."

"Where are you going?" Leach inquired. Behind Joe, Frank was now writing in a memo pad.

"First I'm picking up Mr. Z at nine o'clock," McCafferty said. "Then the two of us will fly to Mexico. I'll probably stay there awhile, and Z will take the full set of plans to sell overseas."

"Why don't you leave sooner?" Leach asked, nervously denting his can.

"Wish I could," McCafferty answered. "But Z said he won't be ready till then. So I'll just live it up tonight in Death Valley, then take off bright and early. Don't worry, Leach, those plans will be out of the country before anybody knows anything."

"Better be," Leach grumbled.

Just then McCafferty turned and looked straight at the pantry door. Joe pulled his face away from the crack, hoping he hadn't been seen.

"Okay, let's get out of here," McCafferty said, putting a few bills on the table. Then he and Leach walked out of the café.

The Hardys could hear Astro-Surfer say goodbye to the two men, then heard two engines start up and drive away.

"Frank," Joe said, stepping out of the pantry, "it sounds like the bald guy was stealing secret information from the Palmdale base!"

Before Frank could respond, Astro-Surfer came back inside and collected the bills from the table. "Sir, can we use your phone?" Joe asked urgently.

"Sorry, it doesn't work." Astro-Surfer shrugged. "The phone company's coming any day now. So they say. There's a phone booth about ten miles south on the interstate, though. How did your surprise go?"

"Perfect," Joe said, already pushing past the squeaky screen door.

"Thanks a lot," Frank said, following Joe.

Seeing no one outside, the Hardys ran to their dirt bikes, kick started their engines, and went blazing across the desert toward the road.

"So McCafferty is our bad guy," Joe called as he drove. "But why would he be involved in stealing top secret plans from the air force?"

"In a way it makes sense," Frank called back.

"His eyesight went a little bad, so the air force made him stop flying. From what McCafferty told us, flying those F-16s was the best part of his life."

"So maybe he felt like taking revenge on the air force," Joe said as the two bikes reached the road.

"Right," Frank agreed. "And because he was dishonorably discharged from the force, he couldn't get a high-paying job with a commercial airline. I guess he figured he could make a bundle off the stolen plans."

"But, you know," Joe called, "I don't see how this has anything to do with Ian Fairbanks."

Hearing an engine revving behind him, Frank jerked around. "Look out!" Frank shouted.

Looking back, Joe saw two vehicles come roaring out of the dark mouth of a cavern. One was Leach's Range Rover and the other was McCafferty's truck!

The Hardys gunned their engines and swerved off the road. The Rover and truck both sped up and began pursuing the Hardys across the rough desert floor.

"He must have seen me through the cracked door," Joe yelled. "Then he waited to ambush us!"

"I think our bikes have the advantage if we stay off the road!" Frank shouted.

"Split up!" Joe called. "Better chance."

Instantly Frank veered one way and Joe veered the other. Leach's Range Rover kept after Joe, and McCafferty's truck continued after Frank.

As Frank turned his handlebar throttle full-on, he heard the engine gun louder and felt the bike pick up speed. He glanced over his shoulder and was glad to see he was putting distance between his bike and McCafferty's truck.

But when Frank faced front again he realized that his flight from the known enemy had only brought him closer to an unseen danger.

He was headed straight for the sheer drop-off of a gaping crater!

12 Most Secret Black

Frank jerked his bike so hard to the right that it flew out from under him. He went crashing to the ground, just short of the crater. Frank sprang up immediately but winced when a sharp pain shot up his right leg.

The red truck screeched to a stop right beside Frank, and McCafferty leaped out of it.

"How about another chop!" McCafferty yelled as he landed a hard karate chop to the back of Frank's neck. Frank had no time to respond. He instantly crumpled to the ground, unconscious.

By now Joe was roaring back around to help Frank, Leach following in the Range Rover. "Should have left him," McCafferty called to Joe.

"Not a chance!" Joe cried, jumping off his bike. He lunged for McCafferty, but the pilot delivered a hard blow to Joe's stomach. Joe's fist shot into McCafferty's chin, but McCafferty managed to catch hold of Joe's arm. Twisting Joe's arm backward, McCafferty forced Joe to the ground and sat on him.

"Get the rope from my truck," McCafferty shouted to Leach. "I'd shoot them but I gave my Berreta away as a Christmas present." Joe knew he was talking about the pistol that had been planted in Frank's bag at the airport.

A few minutes later, Frank and Joe were lying on the ground, bound hand and foot. Joe was wrestling with his rope as Frank finally came to.

"I don't know how much they know," Joe heard McCafferty telling Leach. "But we'd better get rid of them. And we need to put them somewhere where they won't be found. A lot of planes fly over this desert."

"Are you sure we need to, uh . . ." Leach asked.

"Kill them?" McCafferty said. "You bet."

"Well, then, I know the perfect place," Leach said. "The pipeline to Dreamland."

"Beautiful," McCafferty said. "I'll put the bikes in my truck and park it in that cavern we hid in. Then we'll all take a nice drive in the Rover to the pipeline. How far is it?"

"About a hundred and forty miles," Leach said.

Fifteen minutes later, the foursome was driving down the highway in the Range Rover. Leach was at the wheel with Joe seated next to him, while Frank and McCafferty rode in the backseat.

The setting sun began casting long, twisted shadows off the Joshua trees. Frank and Joe rode in silence, each struggling secretly with his ropes, but without much success.

"What are you stealing plans to?" Frank finally asked, breaking the silence.

"Forget it," McCafferty scoffed.

"Oh, come on," Frank insisted. "We've got a long drive ahead of us. Then my brother and I are going to be stuffed inside some sort of pipeline to nowhere. The least you can do is entertain us on the way."

"Good point," McCafferty said with his winning smile. "All right, we'll tell you the whole thing. Call it the story of Mr. X, Y, and Z."

"Nice title," Joe commented from up front.

Frank noticed McCafferty was now acting more like the friendly pilot he had first met.

"A little over a year ago," McCafferty began, "I was in L.A. One night in a club, I met Mr. Leach and we got to talking. He's a fuel specialist for Lockwell, an aeronautical company that does a lot of work for the air force. Leach has been working ten years on a top secret project over at the Palmdale facility."

"What's the project?" Joe asked.

"A top secret airplane," McCafferty confided. "So far they've completed just one of these planes and they're test flying it at a base in Nevada."

"It's the fastest airplane ever," Leach boasted. "It flies six times the speed of sound. Hypersonic."

113

"So the force isn't just *researching* hypersonic," Joe said. "They've already got it."

"I guess that's what Jamal meant by the rumors," Frank said, recalling his friend's comment to General Radman back at Andrews Air Force Base.

Darkness was settling over the desert and Joe felt the air turning cooler. Earlier the Rover had passed several small towns and gas stations, but now there were no signs of civilization along the road.

"Anyway," McCafferty continued, removing his sunglasses, "Leach was mad about being passed over for a promotion, and I've been mad at the force ever since they booted me out. So Leach and I started joking about how we should steal some designs from this top secret plane. After a while we stopped joking and got serious. We realized we could do it. And get rich, too."

"The security is pretty tight at Palmdale," Joe said, remembering the police surrounding him.

"Everything about the plane is the very highest level of top secret," Leach said. "The government calls this level of secrecy 'most secret black.' It's so secret that the Lockwell workers on the project are kept partially in the dark. They are only privy to the details in their field of specialization. But since I was one of the leading fuel experts, and since fuel affects every part of the plane, I had access to every aspect of the plane's design."

"So you managed to sneak out all sorts of designs of the plane," Frank said. "Designs that were designated 'most secret black.' How?"

114

"They don't let you photocopy any documents," Leach said, "so I would study a group of documents, then write them down from memory when I got home. A difficult process, believe me. And an enormous risk. I could get life in prison."

"In other words," McCafferty put in, "he wanted big bucks in advance. Well, I barely make enough to scrape by, so I needed to find someone real wealthy to finance the operation. Finally I did."

"So there were three of you involved," Frank remarked. "Mr. X, Y, and Z."

"That's right," McCafferty nodded. "Every two months Leach, alias X, would gather a collection of secret information. Then Y, that's me, would fly to California and get it. In return, I would give X a sum of money from our financier, Z, keeping a percentage for myself, of course. Then I would give the plans to Z."

"And when Z has all the plans," Joe guessed, "he'll sell them, probably to foreign governments."

"You got it," McCafferty confirmed. "On this trip Leach gave me the sixth and final batch of plans. When Z gets these, he can sell the complete set to the countries that bid the highest."

"I'm confused about something," Joe said. "Did you sabotage the plane Ian Fairbanks was on?"

"I did," McCafferty stated, as if he were impressed with himself. "In Bayport I put two time delay bombs in the plane so it would go down right about where it did. The front bomb blew the engine and radio, the back bomb blew the ELT."

As he stared out of the window and into the dark desert night, Frank began to see the perfection of McCafferty's plan. "I get it now," Frank said slowly. "You weren't trying to kill Ian Fairbanks in that airplane. You were trying to kill Ben Hawkins!"

"Very good," McCafferty said, smiling again.

"But why kill Mr. Hawkins?" Joe wondered.

"Here's why," Frank stated. "Every two months McCafferty would fly out west to get a set of plans from Leach. But he didn't want anyone knowing about the trips so he invented Dexter Cross. Cross posed as a businessman who chartered a flight from Hawkins Air every two months."

"So you would fly Cross somewhere on the east coast," Joe realized, "then fly out west on a commercial flight under a fake name and make your transaction with Leach. Then you'd fly back east and bring Cross back to Bayport."

"And if any suspicion ever fell on you," Frank finished, "the flight records would show you were on the east coast the whole time."

"Excellent," McCafferty confirmed. "You do good work, Hardy."

"But who was Dexter Cross really?" Joe asked.

"Just an out-of-work flight mechanic," said McCafferty. "Never crunched a number in his life. His name's Dave Nelson. Nelson desperately needed money so I hired him to play Cross. He knew I was doing something illegal but had no idea

116

what. He got a little nervous when I told him I had some kids on my trail."

"So Cross, I mean Nelson, was just killing time at the Smithsonian Air and Space Museum in D.C.," Joe said. "But your warning had him worried enough to notice I was following him."

"We also gave Nelson a big payment to keep his mouth shut for the rest of his life," McCafferty added. "In fact, I think he flew out of the country for a nice long vacation this morning."

"That's why we saw him at the airport," Frank said, remembering seeing Cross without his glasses.

"But I still don't see why you sabotaged Mr. Hawkins's plane," Joe told McCafferty.

"Mr. Hawkins had become suspicious of Cross and was planning to investigate," Frank reminded Joe. "Mr. Hawkins could have ruined everything, so McCafferty needed to get rid of him."

"I could have done something simple like shoot him," McCafferty said, "but then there would be a police investigation, and I didn't want that."

"So you fixed his plane to crash when he was on a flight with Ian Fairbanks," Frank explained. "That way everyone, including us, would think someone had been trying to kill Fairbanks, a man with countless enemies. Ben Hawkins was the real target. Fairbanks just made a nice cover story."

"I see," Joe nodded. "Pretty clever."

"And it almost worked," McCafferty said. "But then you boys and Jamal began sniffing around

117

Cross. I couldn't have that, so I followed you to Cross's house and fixed the brakes on your van. No one would question a car accident on a snowy night. But when that didn't kill you, I was afraid you might follow Cross to D.C. And sure enough, I found your plane at the D.C. airport. So I cancelled my meeting with Leach and rescheduled it for today, my next day off. I wanted to make sure you boys were dead before I flew west as Pat Buchman."

"So you were the one who tampered with the carb-heat control on the Cessna," Frank said. "Then you flew Cross back to Bayport a day early. A few kids crashing in a Cessna. That would make sense, too."

"Too bad you accidentally dropped your ticket by the Cessna," Joe remarked. "A ticket that had your new rendezvous time and place scrawled on it."

"So that's how you found me," McCafferty said, slapping his knee. "I was starting to think the two of you were psychic! I didn't realize the ticket was missing till I got back to Bayport. But I figured it was just blowing in the wind somewhere so I bought another one for the same flight."

"No wonder you were so surprised to see me that night in the hangar," Frank said. "I should have been at the bottom of the ocean by then."

"I could have killed you that night," McCafferty said, "but by that time Joe and Jamal were in Plattsburgh and old man Hawkins was okay."

"So you thought a little misdirection wouldn't hurt," Frank said. "You turned out the lights and made it seem as if there was another bad guy in the hangar. You even cut your own cheek with a knife as a cover."

"Ouch," Leach said from up front.

"All in a day's work," McCafferty replied.

"How did you get the gun into my bag at the airport?" Frank asked.

"Finally, I had some luck," McCafferty said. "I was carrying a gun in case I ran into trouble. But when I got to the airport for my flight to L.A., I realized I couldn't take the piece through the metal detector. Then I saw you guys in the ticket line. I just knew you kids were on my trail, so I bought a gift box and ribbon, put the gun inside, and waited for a chance to slip it in your bag."

"I guess the airport was crowded enough to do it without my noticing," Frank said.

"Even better," McCafferty said. "You left your bag for a second when you got in the shoving match with that ugly chauffeur. I knew the gun would keep you off any flights for that day at least."

"But lucky for us," Frank said, "we managed to catch a ride west in a couple of air force F-16s."

"Oh, yeah?" McCafferty said with surprise. "How did you like it?"

"Just like you described it," Joe replied. "Totally awesome."

It was around ten o'clock when Leach finally stopped somewhere past the Nevada border.

119

"Destination achieved," McCafferty announced.

"Oh, goody," Joe said sarcastically.

McCafferty and Leach pulled the Hardys out of the Rover. Frank and Joe looked around—and saw nothing. There was absolutely nothing there except darkness, the distant shape of a mountain range, and a massive black fuel tank several yards away.

"What's the tank for?" Frank asked, wanting as much information about their location as possible.

"The tank feeds into a brand-new pipeline," Leach said, moving to something on the ground resembling a manhole. "The pipeline was just laid, so it's not in use yet."

"What will it feed into?" Frank asked.

"About fifty miles away," Leach explained, pulling a long key from his pocket, "beyond those mountains, there's an extremely secret air force base. The pipes will feed hydrogen fuel to the base for use in the hypersonic planes."

"Why is the tank so far from the base?" Joe asked.

"Hydrogen fuel," Leach explained, "is highly explosive. So it's stored in the absolute middle of nowhere. And that's exactly where you are, kid. Nowhere."

Leach inserted the key in the manhole, turned it, and pulled open the round hatch cover. Frank saw that the cover was a very thick slab of metal.

McCafferty led Frank over to the manhole, Frank stumbling because of the rope around his ankles. Frank looked into the opening and saw a ladder

120

leading down into pitch darkness. Then Leach walked Joe over to the manhole.

"Guys," McCafferty said in an amiable tone, "I'm not happy about this. But I'm not going to prison for the rest of my life either, so . . ." He shrugged, then continued. "You'll be sealed in there pretty good, and I guess you'll die of thirst. Not the most pleasant way to go, and I'm sorry about that."

"How considerate," Frank scoffed.

"Down you go, kid," McCafferty told Frank. "You can't use the ladder with your hands tied behind you, so you'll have to jump."

Frank thought of resisting but knew it was useless with his arms and legs tied. He knelt down, then eased himself into the opening. He swung his legs into the hole and jumped, careful to spring with his feet on landing.

Frank found himself crouched in a large, curving pipe five feet in diameter. A moment later, Joe dropped down beside him.

"So long," the Hardys heard McCafferty call from above. Then the hatch cover clanged shut and they heard the sound of a metal bolt locking them in.

For a few long moments, the brothers sat on the bottom of the pipe, wondering what to do next.

Joe took a very deep breath. The pipe was dark and silent as a tomb—a silence he felt creeping slowly through his skin into his bones.

"Maybe we could yell for help," Joe suggested.

"We're inside a pipe in the middle of a desert," Frank said. "Who would hear us?"

"We're stuck in here for good, aren't we?" Joe asked after a moment.

When Frank didn't answer, Joe took that as a very bad sign.

13 Whisper in the Desert

"Okay," Frank said finally. "There has to be some way out of here. Let me think."

"While you're thinking," Joe said, "I'll work on your ropes."

"Be my guest," Frank said, turning and holding out his wrists.

Joe chewed and tugged and wrestled at Frank's ropes with his teeth. Finally Frank was able to work his hands free.

"Guess you were hungry," Frank joked as he untied Joe's wrists. Then Frank and Joe each undid the ropes around their ankles.

"I say we head toward the tank," Frank said as he started moving through the darkness in the direction of the aboveground tank, which was several yards down the pipe. "There's bound to be some sort of opening there for the fuel."

Joe felt along the pipe but found no break in its smooth surface. A moment later he heard Frank banging his hand against the metal. "Any luck?" Joe called.

"There's an opening," Frank reported, "but it's sealed shut. Why don't we start walking toward the base? Maybe there's a way out at that end."

"Except it's fifty miles away," Joe growled.

"Think of it as a workout," Frank said.

For two long and awful hours, Frank and Joe moved through the complete darkness of the pipe's curved interior. They had to stay crouched down the entire time, and before long their backs and necks and shoulders were hurting like crazy. They both sat down to rest their aching muscles, realizing they'd worked up a thirst and had no way to quench it. The situation was looking dire, and for a long moment they both just lay there, panting.

"It'll take us a week to get to the base," Joe finally said. "We won't last that long, Frank."

"Wait," Frank whispered. "Do you see something on the side of the pipe?"

Joe looked where Frank was pointing and saw two yellow eyes gleaming at him. By now, Joe's eyes were accustomed to the darkness, and he could make out the shape of a long reptile. "It's some sort of a big lizard," Joe whispered. "How did it get in here?"

"That's what I'm wondering," Frank said. "If a

124

lizard crawled in, maybe we can crawl out. There could be another one of those hatchways coming up that's partly open. After all, the pipeline's not in use yet. Come on, bro, let's keep moving."

Forty minutes later the Hardys came to a hatchway similar to the one they had used to enter the pipe. Frank climbed quickly up the ladder and reached for the metal cover.

"I feel air coming through," Frank cried. "I think it's partially . . ." With a grunt, Frank pushed up, and to his great relief, the cover lifted!

"Thank you, Mr. Lizard!" Joe shouted.

Frank hoisted himself out of the hatchway, and Joe wasted no time scrambling out after him. The Hardys fell to the desert floor and stretched their cramped bodies. The air was much cooler now, and Frank was glad he was still wearing his windbreaker.

"Man, it feels good to be out of there," Joe said, reaching his arms upward. A full moon glowed in the sky, and the stars glimmered so brightly that Joe felt he could easily grab one.

"It's one A.M.," Frank said, checking his watch. "Why don't we keep heading toward the base? It'll be light in several hours, and maybe then we'll find a road. I doubt we'll be able to stop McCafferty, but there must be some way to get out of this desert."

For the next three hours, the Hardys trudged through the dark desert. There was nothing but flat, endless land, and the occasional slithering of a reptile or flap of an owl's wings. The boys kept moving toward the distant shape of the mountain range, where they knew the base was, though it never seemed to get any closer.

"Every bone in my body aches from crouching in that pipe," Joe complained.

"And my feet," Frank added. "They feel like—"

KABOOM!

Suddenly there was an explosion so loud it seemed to rip open the sky. As the earth shook, Frank and Joe dove to the ground and covered their heads. A moment later the earth stopped trembling.

"What was that?" Joe asked, raising his head. "An earthquake?"

"Maybe the hydrogen fuel tank blew up," Frank said, scanning the distance for flames.

Then the Hardys heard a low-pitched whispering sound overhead. As the sound grew louder, Frank and Joe both looked up. A stream of smoke was trailing across the glow of the moon. The smoke resembled the contrail of a jet airplane except that it was shaped like a rope running through a long series of doughnuts. Moments later the whispering died away.

Soon the bizarre contrail faded into nothing.

"It must have been some kind of plane," Frank guessed. "Either that or an alien spaceship."

"Hey, I think I see something coming," Joe said, peering into the darkness. "Maybe it's just a Joshua tree and I'm starting to hallucinate."

But Frank thought he could make something out,

126

too, as he peered into the nothingness. "You're right, Joe. Someone, or some *thing*, is coming at us. But what kind of creature of the night would be wandering out here in the middle of nowhere?"

"Could be McCafferty or Leach," Joe said. "But we're not even on a road."

The figure got closer. Frank and Joe stopped, both ready to take off into the desert at the first sign of danger.

Frank saw that the person wore a one-piece dark-colored suit and carried something unidentifiable in his hand. As the figure got closer Frank saw that his eyes were huge and shiny. Maybe I've been away from civilization too long, he thought to himself. Either those are very weird goggles or I'm looking into the eyes of an alien.

Soon the figure came right up to the Hardys. The person lifted the strange goggles, revealing a weathered human face. "Don't I know you?" the newcomer asked.

"Astro-Surfer!" Frank gasped, realizing it was the proprietor of the Oasis café.

"What are you doing out here," Joe asked.

"I was watching that airplane," Astro-Surfer said in his gruff voice. "That's why I've got these infrared goggles on. They let me see in the dark."

"So it *was* an airplane," Frank said. "That must have been a sonic boom we heard."

"Hey," Joe asked excitedly, "was that the hypersonic plane the air force is supposed to have?"

"That's exactly what it was." Astro-Surfer

grinned and looked up at the moon. "They just took it out for a little test-fly. They take it up only at night so no one can get a real good look at it."

"I guess the details of the plane are pretty secret," Joe remarked.

"Secret's not even the word for it," Astro-Surfer replied. "They keep the plane at a base beyond those mountains. And that base is so secret, it's not even on the map. It doesn't even have an official name. It's got a nickname, though . . . Dreamland."

"If all this stuff is so secret, how do you know about it?" Frank asked, wondering what this odd character was up to.

"Oh, there have been rumors about this plane for years." Astro-Surfer chuckled. "And there's a number of crazy people like me roaming the desert at night just for a glimpse of it. Call it a hobby."

"Do you have a Jeep or truck?" Joe asked, eager to get moving.

"Got a Jeep about four miles from here," Astro-Surfer said. "I left it by a road so I wouldn't scar the desert. Can I give you boys a ride somewhere?"

The Hardys instantly accepted the offer. Astro-Surfer gave them water from the flask he was carrying, then began leading them through the darkened desert toward his Jeep. "I told you what I'm doing out here," Astro-Surfer said. "Now it's your turn."

The Hardys exchanged a look. Could they trust this guy? From the looks of things, Frank realized,

Astro-Surfer was their only chance. Frank nodded at Joe, and Joe explained the story of X, Y, and Z as the trio kept walking.

"We've got to get to a phone," Astro-Surfer said after hearing the whole story. "Someone needs to stop this McCafferty fellow. Or better yet, follow him to Mr. Z somehow, before he gets the rest of the designs. You've got no idea who Z is, do you?"

"No," Joe said. "It's obviously someone with a lot of money. And not a lot of scruples."

"Wait a second," Frank said, stopping in his tracks. "I know who Mr. Z is."

"Who is it?" Joe asked, also stopping.

"Ian Fairbanks!" Frank said emphatically. "Think about it. He's very rich and very ruthless. And he desperately needs big money to stop his daughter from taking over his corporation."

"That could be why the payments to Dexter Cross were from a subsidiary of the Fairbanks Corporation," Joe figured.

"And maybe it wasn't an accident that Fairbanks was on the flight that crashed," Frank continued. "Jamal said his dad hardly ever flies clients, but Fairbanks chartered a flight when all the other pilots were booked. McCafferty could have told him when to do it. And remember Mr. Hawkins said he hit his head on something right before the plane crashed? Maybe Fairbanks knocked Mr. Hawkins out."

"And Fairbanks had a parachute," Joe recalled.

"I'll bet anything he had some plan to get out of

those mountains," Astro-Surfer added. "And another plan for selling those top secret plane designs."

"It's bizarre, but in a way it all makes perfect sense," Frank said. "The more I think about it, the more I'm sure of it. Mr. Z is Ian Fairbanks!"

"Frank," Astro-Surfer whispered suddenly. "Don't move, son. There's a big ol' rattlesnake only inches away from your right foot. And those fangs'll go right through your shoe."

Frank turned his head slowly and saw the rattlesnake coiled in a glint of moonlight. The rattle on the snake's tail shook slightly, sending out a menacing buzz that acted like a shot of adrenaline on Frank. Then, in the blink of an eye, the snake uncoiled and struck at Frank!

14 Man Without a Country

Frank twisted away in a spin. With a pounding heart, he turned to see the snake slithering across the desert floor, fast as lightning.

"Nice move," Astro-Surfer said, obviously impressed. "Not many people can outmaneuver a snake."

"My brother's pretty slippery himself," Joe said.

"We'd better keep moving," Astro-Surfer said, glancing at the night sky. "The stars are fading and we're a long way from a telephone."

Astro-Surfer, Frank, and Joe started walking through the desert at a faster pace. "Why are you so interested in protecting this plane?" Frank asked.

"Back in the 1940s," Astro-Surfer explained, "I was a test pilot for the air force. I was one of the first loonies to fly supersonic, so naturally I'm interested in the next wave—hypersonic. They say that plane goes six times the speed of sound. Imagine! That's a mile per second, boys!"

"How long has the air force had this hypersonic plane?" Joe asked.

"They've been testing it out of Dreamland for about three years now," Astro-Surfer explained. "I've heard they've got most of the bugs out, and they're building a whole fleet of them at Palmdale."

"What is the plane's purpose?" Frank asked.

"It's a reconnaissance plane," Astro-Surfer said. "It will fly over other countries and take pictures so we know what those countries are up to. The hypersonic speed is a big advantage because it means the plane can be anywhere on the face of the earth in several hours. That's helpful in a dangerous situation. Even better, that plane could stop such a situation from starting in the first place. That's why the government has spent billions on it and why they've worked so hard to keep its design a secret."

Thirty minutes later the trio came to Astro-Surfer's beat-up Jeep, which was parked along a narrow road that seemed to lead to nowhere. The sky was now shaded with gray, and the stars were flickering dimly.

"I'm sure you fellas need this," Astro-Surfer said, handing the boys a paper bag of sandwiches and a canteen. "Now, here's the problem. It took us longer than I thought to get here. It's six-thirty now. McCafferty said he was taking off from Widow's Dry Lake at seven-thirty, but I don't think we can get to a phone much before then."

"He said he's picking up Mr. Z at nine," Frank said, chewing hungrily on a bologna sandwich. "But we have no idea where."

"Widow's Dry Lake is forty-five minutes from here," Astro-Surfer explained. "There's no phone there either, but if we get there before he takes off maybe we can stop him."

"Even if we stop McCafferty, Fairbanks will still be able to get away with the first five installments of the plans," Frank pointed out. "That's probably enough to build one of those planes."

For a few moments the two boys and the old pilot stared across the vast and desolate expanse of desert, wondering what to do, how far to go.

"This is important," Joe said, watching a star flicker in the sky. "Not only have these guys tried to kill a lot of people, including us, they're threatening the peace of the world."

"Okay," Frank said firmly. "I've got a plan."

"Then let's hit the road," Astro-Surfer said, opening the door to the Jeep.

Forty-five minutes later, the Hardys were hiding behind a cluster of Joshua trees, watching the glowing sun rise over the mountain range. An early morning mist hung in the air.

Several hundred yards in front of the Hardys, an old cargo plane stood alone on a dry lake bed. The plane was dented, and its paint was flaking off.

Soon McCafferty appeared in the Range Rover. He parked near the plane and stepped out of the vehicle, wearing his trademark leather jacket and sunglasses and carrying the satchel Leach had given him at the café. Then the pilot began walking around the plane, checking it over.

"Hey!" Astro-Surfer called, jogging up alongside McCafferty. "I got my Jeep stuck in a crater just yonder. Could you lend an old pilot a hand?"

McCafferty glanced up suspiciously. Astro-Surfer wore a cap pulled low so McCafferty wouldn't recognize him from the Oasis.

"Sure," McCafferty said after sizing him up.

From their hiding place, the Hardys watched McCafferty follow Astro-Surfer toward the Jeep, which they had just carefully wedged into a crater.

Frank and Joe made a dash for the cargo plane and climbed inside. There were two seats in front of an open and roomy cabin. In the back of the plane were old metal supply boxes and an assortment of tools. There was also a tarpaulin, and the Hardys slipped under it to hide.

From underneath the tarp the Hardys watched McCafferty climb into the plane, toss the satchel at his feet, and start up the plane's outdated engine. The Hardys felt the plane roll down the desert and eventually lift up into the air.

After an hour of waiting silently under the tarp, the Hardys heard McCafferty talking to himself.

"Let's see," the pilot said loudly over the noisy drone of the plane. "I should be at the store in Palm Springs in about twenty minutes. I land in the desert by the parking lot, I pick up the big man, and then we're off to sunny Mexico!"

Joe realized "the store in Palm Springs" probably meant a Fairbanks department store.

"And I am now officially el richo!" McCafferty crowed. Then he began singing the air force song as he flew the plane. "'Off we go into the wild blue yonder!'" he bellowed. "'Riding high into the sky!'"

As McCafferty sang gleefully, he pulled back on the control lever and sent the plane steeply upward. The Hardys felt themselves rolling, but they braced themselves against the fuselage, trying not to make much noise. Next, the plane arced and started sloping steeply downward.

Suddenly the metal boxes and several tools went tumbling noisily across the cabin floor. Unfortunately, so did the Hardys. McCafferty spun around and glared through his sunglasses at the boys.

"Hi, there," Frank said, unsure what to do next.

"You guys are like cockroaches!" McCafferty cried in amazement. "You just don't die!"

"Not when there's a crazy traitor flying around," Joe said, rising and moving unsteadily toward the pilot. "Why don't you give up, McCafferty? We've got you outnumbered."

"Oh, I imagine it would be a pretty even fight."
McCafferty grinned. "But then we'd probably
crash in the sand before it was over."

Frank realized the pilot was right. A fight in a
flying airplane would leave no winners.

"Listen," Frank said, attempting a sympathetic
manner. "Even if you got away with those plans,
you would never be able to come back to the United
States. This is your home, Ken. Everyone and
everything you know is here. Can you really turn
your back on it forever?"

Keeping a hand on the control lever, McCafferty
looked at the Hardys through his sunglasses. He
seemed momentarily confused, pained, perhaps
weighing what Frank had just said.

Then the pilot reached down and picked up a
long wrench that had rolled to the front of the
plane. He rose from his chair, leaving the controls.

"This country wasn't good to me." McCafferty
spoke with growing intensity. "This country turned
its back on *me*. The force decided I couldn't fly
anymore and then they threw me out. I don't care if
I never see this country again. I have no country!"

McCafferty bashed madly at the radio with the
wrench, smashing the plastic device. The pilot's
sunglasses flew off his face, and the Hardys saw an
expression of rage flashing in his green eyes.

"The air force took something away from me!"
McCafferty yelled. "And now I'm taking something
away from them." He lifted the wrench high and
swung it violently down on the control lever over

and over, the plane rocking wildly back and forth as he did.

"Stop him!" Frank shouted, struggling for balance. But as he and Joe moved toward the pilot, they were both knocked over by the rocking plane.

"And I'm going to be rich!" McCafferty yelled as he began smashing the plane's second control lever. Soon both levers were knocked completely off their rods, and the plane was bucking like a wild bronco.

"Okay, fellas," McCafferty said, breathing hard. "You want the plane? It's yours. Only thing is, it doesn't fly too well."

Then McCafferty scooped up a parachute pack that was on the floor and slung it around one shoulder.

"Wait," Joe urged as he stepped forward.

"Stay back!" McCafferty yelled, swinging the long wrench at Joe. Then the pilot grabbed the satchel and backed toward the plane's door. He kicked the plane door open, and a sharp gust of wind blew through the cabin.

"You'll be caught," Frank called, trying not to show the extent of his fear. "Stay and help me land the plane and we'll help you get off easier."

"No way!" McCafferty yelled over the rushing wind. "I'll be a little late for my rendezvous with Mr. Z, but I'll get there. I guarantee it. As for you guys, well, adios, cockroaches!"

McCafferty gave a firm salute. Then he clamped the satchel handle between his teeth and jumped out of the plane. Joe ran to the door and watched the pilot plummet through the air. A moment later the parachute billowed open, and McCafferty was floating safely toward the ground.

Just then the plane began diving downward. Joe grabbed the doorframe to keep from falling out and plummeting to a certain death. As the wind roared against his face, he saw the sandy brown surface of the desert rushing closer and closer.

"Do something!" Joe demanded. "We're crashing!"

"I've got no control device!" Frank yelled, pulling himself off the cabin floor.

As the plane dove downward, Joe glanced out the door again. His stomach somersaulted as he saw the harsh desert floor rushing up to meet them!

15 Dreamland

"It's time to remember what Jamal told us," Frank said, struggling not to panic.

"What's that?" Joe cried.

"If you stay cool, you can usually save the day."

"A steering wheel wouldn't hurt either!" Joe yelled back. He figured they were less than a minute from crash-and-burn status.

But Frank was already in the pilot's chair, scanning the ancient instrument panel. He yanked the throttle knob and pulled up the flap lever. Instantly, Frank could feel they weren't diving as fast.

"I've slowed us down," Frank said, his mind searching for more ideas. "Let's see, there's no autopilot, but . . . maybe I can level us off with the elevator trim." Frank began rotating a large notched wheel. But the plane kept diving.

"Hurry!" Joe called from the door. He could see the desert rushing closer every second.

Frank rotated the wheel all the way back and held his breath for a very tense fifteen seconds. Then the plane began leveling. It was flying low, but it was definitely flying.

"Yes!" Frank cheered.

Joe slammed the door shut, cutting off the sharp wind. "Are we okay?" Joe asked hopefully.

"For now," Frank said. "Except we can't guide the plane and we can't land it."

"That's a problem," Joe noted. "As soon as we run out of fuel, we'll go down again. And we can't radio for help because McCafferty bashed the radio with the—"

"The wrench!" Frank exclaimed. He picked up the long wrench that McCafferty had used to destroy the control levers. "Maybe we can use the wrench to control the plane."

Frank knelt down and tightened the wrench onto a broken rod that had once been attached to one of the control levers. "Now, if I ease it back . . ." Frank said, pulling back on the rod with the wrench.

Gradually the plane nosed upward.

"It works!" Frank called. "And the rudder pedals should be okay. With a lot of luck, we might be able to control this thing enough to land it."

"Nice work, Frank," Joe said, sitting in the copilot's chair. "We should be pretty close to Palm Springs by now. Let's try to get there before

140

McCafferty does. We want to get to Fairbanks first. Otherwise, he may scram with the first five installments of the plans."

"Maybe you're right," Frank said, keeping his hand on the wrench. "McCafferty said there was a place to land near the parking lot of the store."

"Here's a map," Joe said, picking a map off the floor and studying it. "If we keep heading southwesterly, we should hit Palm Springs soon."

"It'll be easy to spot," Frank said. "It's where every house has a swimming pool."

Working together, Frank and Joe flew the crippled plane. Within fifteen minutes the lonely desert below gave way to an oasis of elegant homes.

"There's Palm Springs!" Joe cried, looking out the windshield at the green lawns and blue pools that stood out against the sandy background. Moments later he saw a huge Fairbanks department store. Just beyond the store's parking lot was a stretch of open desert.

"There's plenty of room for us to land without hurting anyone," Joe called.

"Cut back on the throttle," Frank called.

As Joe pulled the throttle knob, Frank pushed forward on the wrench and the plane began angling toward the ground.

"When we hit," Frank called, "shove the brake."

"Hang on!" Joe yelled.

Suddenly the plane banged violently against the ground, bounced up, then banged down again. As the plane rolled across the hard desert floor, Joe shoved down on the rudder pedal with his foot until the plane slowed, then jerked to a stop.

"For the crash of your life," Frank announced, "fly the Hardy Express."

"Let's head for the store!" Joe said, springing from his chair.

Frank and Joe jumped out of the plane and hit the ground running. A few minutes later, they were racing through the store's parking lot, dodging cars.

"Fairbanks is probably hiding in the offices," Joe called as they ran through the lot.

"We'll check there first," Frank called back.

Frank and Joe burst through the store's glass doors. Though it was early Sunday morning, the store was already open and filling with shoppers. Joe thought it was odd to see the Christmas decor contrasting with the shoppers dressed in shorts and summer clothing.

Moving through the store, Frank passed the scarlet figure of Santa Claus, carrying a large bag of presents.

"Ho ho ho!" Santa greeted Frank.

"There's the elevator," Joe said, pulling Frank away from the jolly Santa.

The Hardys rode the elevator to the top floor and got out in a reception area similar to the one in the Bayport store. There was no one there.

"You take the hallway to the right, I'll take the one to the left," Joe ordered.

Frank wasn't moving, though. He was staring at a

portrait of Ian Fairbanks on the wall. It was the same one he had seen in the Bayport store.

"Joe!" Frank cried. "That wasn't Santa Claus down there. It was Ian Fairbanks."

"What?" Joe rushed back to the reception area.

"That Santa Claus had the same dark, bushy eyebrows Fairbanks has in this portrait," Frank said excitedly. "Think about it. Fairbanks was expecting McCafferty, so he would have been keeping watch from his office window. Then he sees us climbing out of the cargo plane instead of McCafferty. He needed some cover fast, so he left his office and put on the Santa outfit. I know it's him, Joe, and I bet he has the first five sets of the stolen plans in his bag."

"You should be a detective!" Joe exclaimed.

The Hardys ran down three flights of escalators to the ground floor and raced back to the spot where Frank had seen the renegade Santa.

"Where is he?" Joe asked, glancing around. "How hard can it be to spot a fat man in a bright red suit?"

"Look, there's his bag!" Frank said, noticing an abandoned bag of presents on the floor.

"And there he goes!" Joe pointed, now seeing Santa running out the front door of the store.

The Hardys fought their way through crowded aisles and busy shoppers until they burst through the glass doors of the store's entrance.

Up ahead the Hardys saw Santa Claus running

through the parking lot, carrying a leather suitcase. He was heading toward a black lightplane. Beyond it, Joe saw the dilapidated cargo plane.

"Where did that plane come from?" Frank yelled.

"Beats me," Joe called back. "But I bet Santa's got the plans in that suitcase. If we call someone now, Fairbanks may be gone for good. We have to stop that plane or get on it!"

The Hardys doubled their pace, and by the time Santa reached the black plane, they were close behind him. The door to the plane flew open, Santa climbed in, and the plane began taxiing across the desert.

"Not without us you don't!" Joe yelled, grabbing onto the door and swinging himself into the plane. Then he hauled Frank into the plane, just as it lifted off the ground.

"What the—" Santa sputtered. "Who are you?"

The pilot's head whipped around at Santa's words, and Joe saw the pilot was none other than Ken McCafferty.

"I don't believe my eyes," McCafferty said, facing forward again as he guided the plane upward.

"Then you better get glasses, pal!" Joe shouted.

"What did you do?" Frank asked McCafferty. "Wave down some plane in the desert, then steal it?"

"That's exactly what I did," McCafferty boasted.

Frank turned to Santa Claus, who had by now pulled off his cap, white wig, and white beard. The portly man before them was definitely the same man in the portrait, bushy eyebrows and all.

"Mr. Fairbanks," Frank said, "we've been looking for you for some time now."

"I'm flattered," Fairbanks said in a British accent. "Ken has been telling me how resourceful you boys have been."

"We could say the same for you," Joe said. "For example, how did you get out of those mountains?"

"Quite simple really," Fairbanks responded. "I parachuted out of the plane, landed, then used a shortwave radio to call for another plane to pick me up. It was all prearranged, of course, and I was safe and warm before anyone knew I was missing."

"Then where did you go?" Frank asked.

"Oh, let's just say I've been in hiding." Fairbanks smiled. "I have so many enemies in the world, I knew the police and the FBI and everybody else would assume someone had tried to assassinate me by sabotaging that plane. They would never suspect it was all a ploy to dispose of Ben Hawkins."

"Are you planning to stay in hiding the rest of your life?" Frank asked, noticing Fairbanks's bag on the floor beside him.

"Certainly not," Fairbanks replied. "After I sell the stolen plans, I'll resurface, explaining that because someone was obviously trying to kill me I thought it wise to stay out of sight for a while. Then it'll be back to business as usual. And I can keep that wily daughter of mine from taking over my empire."

"What should we do with them?" McCafferty asked from up front. "The kids know everything now."

"Fortunately Santa always carries a little something for the more rebellious elves," Fairbanks said. He pulled a pistol from his shiny black belt. "I believe I'll kill the blond one first."

Joe thought the plane's engine might be the last sound he ever heard. But then he felt a gust of wind and saw that the door of the plane was wide open.

"If you want these you'd better not shoot!" Frank said, holding Fairbanks's suitcase out the door.

Joe saw the other satchel lying up front by McCafferty's feet. "And these," Joe said, suddenly grabbing the satchel and holding it out the door.

"Don't you think I have copies of the plans?" Fairbanks said, keeping the pistol on Joe.

"For the first five installments, I'm sure you do," Frank said. "But not for the set that Joe is dangling out the door right now. And how do you plan to get your hands on those copies? We're not the only ones who know what you've been up to. You won't be able to set foot on U.S. soil without being arrested. So these actually *are* your only set."

"So 'ho ho ho' yourself," Joe quipped.

"Hmmm," Fairbanks said. "Even if you're lying, we seem to have a bit of a stalemate, don't we? If I shoot, you drop the plans. If you drop the plans, I shoot. But then in about ten minutes we'll be landing in Mexico. And once we're on the ground, all you can do is drop the plans at my feet. And then I will certainly shoot you."

Frank knew Fairbanks was right. Holding the plans out the window would keep them alive until they got on the ground, but after that they were dead men.

Just then Joe saw something in the clear blue sky. There was another plane not far behind them! Joe leaned out the door and waved frantically. As if the pilot understood, the plane put on speed. Before long the small green plane was directly behind them.

"What are you doing?" Fairbanks demanded. "What's out there?"

Joe watched as the green plane executed an aerobatic design in the air. Then he realized with a growing sense of excitement and relief that the plane was making the letter *J*.

"It's Jamal!" Joe cried with joy. "I don't know how he got here, but it's him!"

The green plane flew around in front of the black plane, blocking McCafferty's path. McCafferty jerked back on the control wheel, attempting to shoot his plane up and over the intruder, but just as fast, Jamal's plane also shot upward.

"Nice one, Jamal!" Joe called, closing the door.

McCafferty pulled his plane into a ferocious full turn, sending the passengers sprawling across the cabin—but then Jamal flew around and cut off McCafferty again.

147

"Get us to Mexico!" Fairbanks ordered. "Now!"

"He's covering me too well!" McCafferty shouted.

"Jamal's a great free safety," Joe said proudly. "And he specializes in interceptions."

The aerial dogfight continued for a dizzying ten minutes. Then the Hardys saw Jamal's plane abruptly peel away. They both wondered why their friend was backing off now.

It wasn't long before they saw the reason. Appearing out of nowhere in the distant sky, the familiar gray shapes of two F-16 fighter planes barreled toward them.

"Here comes the air force!" Frank cheered.

"What'll we do?" Fairbanks shouted.

"It's over," McCafferty said as he glimpsed the F-16s blazing a trail straight toward him. "Those guys are the best flyboys around. I should know. I used to be one of them."

With a look of sadness in his eyes, the ex–air force fighter pilot took his plane into a descent.

Within minutes the planes had landed in the desert and the F-16s were already zooming back into the clouds. Ten state trooper cars were on the scene, and the troopers immediately took custody of McCafferty, Fairbanks,and the two satchels of stolen plans.

As Jamal and the Hardys watched the traitors taken away in handcuffs, a trooper came over to the boys. "We've already picked up Ed Leach," the trooper said. "Some character named Astro-Surfer told us the whole incredible story. Eventually, we believed him."

"Now tell us," Joe demanded of Jamal, "where did *you* come from?"

"I called the Palmdale base last night to check on you guys," Jamal explained. "When they said you had been gone since the afternoon, I figured you were in some trouble and I'd better come looking for you. I flew to L.A. last night and the air force agreed to lend me the green Talon. I spent the morning sweeping the desert for you."

"And I bet you saw McCafferty pushing some poor guy out of the black plane," Frank guessed.

"That's right," Jamal confirmed. "I didn't know what McCafferty was up to, but it didn't look good, so I followed him. He lost me, though, and I radioed the force. Apparently it took them a while to take me seriously, so I kept searching for the plane. Then, when I saw some lunatic leaning out of a plane and waving to me, I figured it must be a Hardy brother."

"We'd be goners without you," Joe admitted.

"The real mystery," Jamal said, putting an arm around each Hardy, "is how you guys have gotten along all this time without me."

That night Frank, Joe, and Jamal found themselves at a place so secret it wasn't on any map— Dreamland. They had been invited there as special guests of the U.S. Air Force, in recognition of their outstanding heroism.

The three were standing on a tarmac, along with about forty air force personnel, waiting for their first glimpse of the hypersonic plane. All around the base, Frank could see an oval range of protective mountains. It was completely dark except for white lights that glowed eerily along a runway.

"So this is Dreamland," Joe said loudly. The boys were all wearing earplugs.

"And there's the dream," Jamal remarked.

A dark shape came gliding out of a gigantic hangar that had a U.S. flag draped in front of it like a curtain. It was the world's first hypersonic airplane. The plane was black and sleek and shaped into a long triangle. The darkness prevented the boys from discerning any other features of the aircraft.

"That'll be in the Smithsonian one day," Frank said as the plane slid past them onto the runway.

The plane had no windshield to see into, but someone the Hardys knew was in the three-man cockpit. "I think it's great the air force decided to let Astro-Surfer go up," Joe commented. "It's only right that one of the pioneers of supersonic flight gets to experience hypersonic."

"There she goes," Jamal called as the plane roared down the runway, faster and faster. With a thunderous rush of sound, the black aircraft lifted effortlessly off the ground.

The three friends peered hard into the sky, but the hypersonic plane was already invisible in the cloak of night. Two seconds later the plane was nothing but a distant whisper.

"Just amazing," Joe said in awe.

"Well, we may not have gotten a Christmas present for Aunt Gertrude," Frank joked, "but I guess we got a pretty big one for Uncle Sam."

Jamal put a finger to his lips and said, "Shhh. It's a secret. You can't tell anyone about this plane, not even Uncle Sam."

Watching the contrails slowly fade in the night sky, Joe said, "What plane?"

NANCY DREW® MYSTERY STORIES By Carolyn Keene

THE HARDY BOYS® SERIES By Franklin W. Dixon